MAYHEM IN AFRICA

Cy Charles Ross

Copyright: CyCharlesRoss©2021

Author: Cy Charles Ross

Published: February 2021

Published by: Independent Publishing Network

Printed by: Shortrun Press

ISBN: 978-1-80049-142-7

All rights reserved. This book may not be reproduced in part or whole by any process without written permission from the copyright holder.

DEDICATION

I dedicate this book to Ursula for her support in writing this book and for the love and laughter we have shared since 1989.

ACKNOWLEDGEMENTS

My grateful thanks go to Jade Baker-Edwards who is my publisher and agent. Also to Lesley Bond, Hazel Tamkin and Sara Baker for their invaluable help with the production of this book.

PREFACE

The adventures of my first book, *Mayhem in France* precede what you are about to read. *Mayhem in Africa* is a complete story in its own right but I do recommend that you read them both. This preface serves to bridge the gap between the two publications.

After life with the French Resistance, I returned to the Fleet Air Arm in England and was posted to the Royal Naval Air Service (RNAS) in Somerset. Later, all personnel at the station were transferred to Lee-on-Solent whilst awaiting transport to fight the Japanese in the Far East.

As you will know from *Mayhem In France*, I was released prematurely from an aircraft maintenance course in order to train for action with the French Resistance. Unfortunately, I was therefore not qualified to work on aircraft and aircraft carriers. So instead of fighting the Japanese, I was posted to RNAS Anthorn and billeted with the Master at Arms and the Regulating Petty Officer. This was possibly with security in mind, to share and enjoy the privileges appertaining to them.

Thereafter, I resumed my civilian life in telecommunications. I studied hard and attended many courses both in Birmingham and at Dollis Hill Research Station in London. Thereafter, I rose to the dizzying heights of being the Senior Telecommunications Officer in both Automatic Telephony and Maintenance Control.

CHAPTER 1

I walked across the tarmac at London airport with a little apprehension and self-doubt. The war had ended a few years ago and everything now seemed so mundane. The danger, excitement and unpredictability experienced throughout the war years had gone out of my life, leaving a fire subdued. I could not settle and was eager to move on.

I had flown previously, but only in a single-engined, high winged Lysander aircraft. This time I was flying to Kenya in a much bigger, modern plane. It would be a much longer journey, but again the unknown awaited me. Mau Mau terrorism was rife in Kenya, and the way of life there was a complete mystery to me. Yet, I smiled inwardly, thinking that this is what I wanted. There is nothing mundane about this situation, but once again… the self-doubt. Had I thought it through? Was I a trifle impetuous? It was too late now for doubt!!

As we roared down the runway, little did I know that I was about to embark on another exciting, dangerous, funny and vastly interesting phase of my life.

I was leaving behind a comfortable life with secure employment as a Senior Technical Officer in telecoms, with a technical responsible post. My first application for overseas employment was with the Shell Oil Company in Abadan, only to be frustrated when the oil fields were nationalised. Nothing daunted, I was well on the way to joining the Government of Sudan, only for a revolution to erupt there! Still hoping for the third time lucky, I pressed on for an appointment with the Colonial Service for service in East Africa and attended for my interview at the Crown Agents in Millbank, London.

I was ushered into an anteroom where about a dozen smartly dressed, tight-lipped men were sitting on straight-backed chairs, clearly awaiting their turn for the interview. A few of them were looking at their feet, others at the wall on which hung a picture of Runnymede. They all looked serious and thoughtful and some gave me a nervous smile as though oblivion was unavoidable. I became one of them. The nervous silence was terrible. If only I had a paper bag!!

To take my mind off the tense environment and forthcoming battle, I weighed up the characters who represented the opposition. Each one was very quiet with his own thoughts. I wondered what they were like at home. What made them tick? How important was this interview to them? How often did they wear such smart suits? Why did they wish to go abroad, and why to Kenya in its unstable state? I was lost in people-watching mode when my in-depth observations were cut as sharply as a knife when the door opened and my name was called.

An angular, obviously efficient, middle-aged secretary showed me into a brightly lit room. Arranged in front of me behind a large, elongated table equipped with neat papers and folders sat the gentlemen about to torture me with their questions and assessment of me.

After initial pleasantries and smiles to show that they were friendly and did not bite, they gestured and invited me to sit down on a very lonesome chair facing them. The first one knew his subject and started at the deep end on technical questions, ably abetted by the second one. This grilling continued in time and detail, and on completion, I felt that I had ably acquitted myself. Then, the various other interviewers present upspoke with family background and social activity questions. A gentleman (who was very obviously tanned by the sun) concerned himself with questions of my relationship with others, and was visibly pleased when I mentioned my amateur dramatics and table tennis prowess. Eventually, it ended with polite smiles all round and I joined the shell-shocked remainder of the opposition. A little later, I was called and led into an office and told I could go home.

Before the month ended there was brilliant news!! I received a letter with an appointment to see a Harley Street doctor for a medical examination. Tightly clutching my specimen bottle, I presented myself at the door of an elite Harley Street physician. A thorough examination ensued by a very mature male doctor. During the procedure, I was required to sit on a chair, one leg over the other, as directed by him. Without any warning, he bent down and tapped my knee to record my reflexes. Consequently, my leg shot up rapidly and hit him in the face. He was visibly annoyed (I think more with himself), and muttered, "Nothing wrong with your reflexes". I could have told him that.

A few weeks later, I was exhilarated to hear that despite the opposition I had been successful! I was appointed to the Colonial Service and duly agreed to the conditions of service. I would be serving with the East African High Commission seconded by the Colonial Office. I must, as a condition of service, pass written and verbal elementary, intermediate and final examinations in Swahili within two years. If I was unable to do this the Colonial Office could terminate the secondment and I could then decide whether to stay in East Africa or return to England and resume my previous occupation.

After medical injections, my air ticket and travel documents were sent to me along with the usual pamphlets and small books of precautions against possible harm to my person whilst in tropical Africa. A wonderful night of merriment was had with my work colleagues and others before I went on my way.

BOAC (now British Airways) offered barley sugar sweets in the 1950s to help combat the effects of altitude change in the ear. Sucking my barley sugar, I settled down and looked forward to the journey ahead. We landed in Rome four hours later after rewarding views of the Alps, The Matterhorn and Mont Blanc which were easily identified. After refreshing ourselves, we, the passengers had to be content with the confines of the transit lounge for one hour whilst aircraft refuelling took place. Following this we left on a seven-hour grind to Cairo in a BOAC Argonaut, flying at 17,000 feet (which was the normal flying altitude in the early 1950s). I was so looking forward to my destination that I was quite willing to leave Cairo and reach Khartoum, hot as hell in Sudan. Five hours after leaving Khartoum, the last part of the tiring flight ended when we landed at Nairobi Airport, 5,450 feet above sea level. To mine and fellow passengers' consternation, the aircraft landed on the port side wheel, shuddered, then stabilised as we hit the muddy extension of the runway. I HAD MADE IT!!

A very friendly individual met me at the airport and took me by car on the long drive to the Queen's Hotel in the centre of Nairobi. The journey from the airport gave me my first glimpses of African villages and their occupants. I witnessed mud huts and lean-to canopies of corrugated iron and other materials. There were native women (some with multicoloured garments), black, shiny skinned men in ragged shorts and children playing as children universally do. The roads and roadside villages so sandy and dusty were the fleeting images as we sped by. My first impressions of Nairobi were the many cars accompanied by their noisy and strident horns, bicycles galore, in surprisingly busy streets. Then, Delamere Avenue, the very wide main street, beautifully lined both sides with exquisitely coloured Jacaranda trees, everywhere seemingly so spacious.

And so, to my first abode in Africa, the main lounge of the Queen's Hotel, 1950s style. Tall African waiters, wearing long white kanzus with broad green belts ghosted amongst the tables.

After using sign language and surreptitiously pointing to bottles on other tables, I managed to purchase a large bottle of the local brew (White Cap Lager), which I thought was a great achievement. The African waiter must have thought he was dealing with a nut case because I discovered later, that they all spoke and understood English perfectly. Most of them had been brought up and educated in missionary schools. The 'Innocents Abroad' was soon brought home to me when I discovered that walking up the wide stairway to get to my room became highly undignified. The high altitude had seriously increased the effect of alcohol on lowland creatures like me after consuming only one litre of lager. On reaching the safety of my room I had a serious battle with the mosquito net before getting into bed. But, with the added assistance from the lager, I slept soundly through the night.

I awoke to a smell, not unpleasant, of charcoal smoke flavoured with God knows what, wafting up through the window. I discovered later that charcoal was the fuel widely used by Africans for cooking. Cocooned in the mosquito net which hung down from the ceiling on a piece of cord, I was lying in a distinctly unknown environment staring at a six inch lizard resting motionless on the wall of my room. How the hell did it stay there? It must have giant suckers on its feet. Do they bite? I had never seen one before; this was life before David Attenborough! Everything seemed so unreal and so strange.

Now fully awake I showered and went down to breakfast. Afterwards, I ventured outside and found the day was not unlike a typical English summer's day. Nairobi was very impressive, with the beautiful Delamere Avenue as previously mentioned. I was taken from the hotel and introduced to new colleagues and surroundings. A relaxing day ensued, drinking in the atmosphere, looking closely at the equipment and conditions, and picking up a few words of Swahili.

Although confident in my engineering capabilities, I had some doubts regarding the new language requirement, so I engaged a professional Swahili teacher by the name of Abdul who was recommended by someone who had already passed this barrier. Abdul and I hit it off immediately which helped enormously.

In the Queen's bar the next evening, I met Paddy. He was to share my room. All rooms had twin beds and it was customary to share a room, especially when accommodation was difficult to come by.

A stocky, amiable character was Paddy, who had been a Japanese prisoner of war. We had dinner together and spent the evening chatting.

We covered a variety of subjects and others joined us at the bar detailing horrific incidents perpetrated by Mau Mau terrorists, and impressing us to be ever on guard. Get a handgun as soon as possible, we were repeatedly advised.

Paddy and I arrived in our room feeling distinctly mellow. I had a problem with my mosquito netting and had just about mastered the technique, being quite sure that every part was tucked well in. I divulged this vital information to Paddy and both of us thought it hilarious. The White Caps and altitude, of course, had a distinct bearing on our attitude.

I was violently propelled from a deep, lager-assisted sleep into an unreal alertness. Paddy was screaming, "They are in the room, they'll kill us for sure!!". Self-preservation being a tried, honed and personal speciality of mine almost shot me out of the bed. I say almost because I immediately became like a fly in a spider's web, enmeshed and tugging at my mosquito netting. Such a stupid thing to tuck it in so tightly — briefly flashed through my mind. Getting out on my feet and going for the intruders was my most urgent need.

I stopped in the middle of this one-sided battle with my netting. It had now dropped down over me and had ensnared me. I stopped because other than my violent thrashing with this netting, complete silence pervaded the room. There was not a soul to be seen except Paddy sitting up in bed, holding his head in his hands. "Sorry, Cy. I've just had a nightmare. I often get these", quote he!

At this early stage of my employment, in simple terms (to save you, my readers, from boring technical paraphernalia), my initial work entailed acceptance testing the equipment that was being installed in the new automatic telephone exchange in Nairobi. Furthermore, I had to assess the functional ability and assets of the experimental equipment that was also being installed. If the latter was deemed to be successful both in Nairobi's climatic conditions (that were normally hostile to telecommunications) and compatible with numerous long line terminations in Kenya, it would be a big step forward to using it elsewhere. So, I was thus employed throughout this period to accustom myself to working with the African, Asian and European employees and to stay until most of the teething problems had been resolved.

This particular period would also be used to become reasonably fluent in basic Swahili, so that decisions regarding my posting to Uganda, Kenya or Tanzania could then be made by the East African High Commission, which administered all three territories. During my private time, I was feverishly learning Swahili (with great help from Abdul) and during the day I was working with many Africans who could speak varying degrees of English, which helped enormously. Or did it?

Whilst in this language mode I found an added difficulty, discovering that time expression was different. Because sunrise was the same time all year round on the equator, 7 am would be 1 am through African eyes, because it is the first hour of the day. I suppose quite logically so! Hence, to express a rendezvous at 8 am in the English language would become 2 am in Swahili (and so on throughout the time cycle remembering the 6-hour difference). The African also had to alter his expression of the time when speaking English so I always confirmed times with them.

It was also deemed beneficial to frame any questions positively in English because their correct missionary education in English meant that an indirect question would have an affirmative answer. For example:

"You didn't get that did you?"

"Yes, sir."

"Are you sure?"

"Yes, sir. I did not get it."

The only way to safeguard one's sanity is to ask a direct question, thus: "Did you get that?". What with Swahili itself, the time expression and the latest anomaly, I had become partially deranged before I realised it.

In the meantime, Paddy had moved on to pastures new. I was left on my own once again, but not for long. My next roommate appeared on the scene. He was nervous, nicely mannered, well turned out and was blessed with quite a thin frame, neck and face to match. I am not being unkind but I felt he could do with eating a few good English roast beef dinners! His name was Alec Horton and he was employed by a firm of auctioneers. He was very conscious of the Mau Mau threat and had been in Nairobi for longer than I had. But above all else, he possessed a car, which I did not!! Although it was an old English car (an Austin), and on the small side, it was still a car. I thought I could make good use of Alec and his car, and perhaps with a little persuasion we could go places and have a look around!

On returning to the hotel room, Alec went across to the window and asked, "Do you mind the window being closed?".

"Why do you want the window closed?"

"Because I sleepwalk."

Oh, God. Not another one! He looked so frail and nervous getting into bed that I felt sorry for him. Of course, by now I considered myself an old hand. The initial antagonism with the net had receded, and although not the best of friends the net and I tolerated each other. I drifted off to sleep, as is my norm, but could be awake at the slightest sound unless my sleep was lager-assisted to a high degree. At about 3 am, a rustling noise started coming from Alec's bed. He got out of bed quite deliberately, easily pushing his net to one side. Then, he stood to attention between the two beds and with his back to me he shouted, "Ford Prefect, Ford Prefect, your rear light is out!".

I said, "And your light will be out if you don't get back into bed!".

CHAPTER 2

I became quite friendly with Alec. The fact that he had means of transport may possibly have helped the friendship along. He never went anywhere in his car, except locally to his place of employment. We managed a few drinks together in the hotel, and other hotels. It was a very low-key existence considering there was so much to see in such a lovely country. Yet I was often tied up with my duties and my Swahili lessons, except for Sundays, when we both had free time. Alec seemed to agree with almost all the suggestions I made as to where we went. He stayed so close to me at times, especially in new places, that I almost fell over him. It was as though I wore some kind of special armour plating with which he wished to share.

When having a drink one evening at the bar I told him that there was a café out of town, near Thika, where one could eat as many cakes as one wished for a total of 50p (East African pence), and that it was only approximately 60 km out of Nairobi. He digested this information quite happily, but when I suggested that perhaps we could go there in his car and that it would be such a lovely change of scene, a gradual look of horror crept up his face.

"Up there, near Thika?", he said with wild eyes. "But there are lots of Mau Mau up there. No one goes there!!"

I said, "That's not a problem. We will be moving on the road, and there is a garrison of Askaris (armed police) at Thika".

He wasn't at all convinced that it was a good idea. I bought him another drink hoping that it would make him a little bolder before I pursued the subject again. I continued to brainwash him during the week but to no avail. After more effort on my part, he was silent for quite some time.

Suddenly he said, "Do you really think it safe to go up there, Cy? Honestly?".

"Of course it will be safe. No problem", I said. "It will do us good to get away somewhere."

By the end of the week, he agreed. I was cock-a-hoop over this! We left Nairobi on Sunday morning. As we turned onto Delamere Avenue, I noticed his knuckle-white grip on the steering wheel and respected his courage for deciding to go, instinctively knowing that he wasn't at all happy with the idea. His face showed great intent and a look of grim determination.

We were well out of Nairobi and I was looking out on the vastness of the landscape, feeling like a bird let out of its cage. There seemed to be not a living soul anywhere. We were completely on our own. How I wished my Mum and Dad and friends at home could see this with me, to share it with them. I was so glad that I had persuaded Alec to come. He seemed to be more relaxed now we were three parts there and became positively chatty. We discussed the wonderful scenery, with Mount Kenya always there in the background and the Ngong Hills beyond Nairobi far behind us to the rear.

Alec was now fully confident and in control. The road was made of loose shale. We were travelling up a slight gradient, the open country dropping away for miles on both sides of the road, when "BANG!". The nearside rear wheel had a puncture. Poor old Alec! This seemingly calmer person, enjoying himself a few minutes ago, suddenly turned into a downcast, worried and concerned individual.

Out came the jack and spare wheel. The jack had to be positioned through the floor of the passenger side of the vehicle, which I found rather odd. I had just got it into position when Alec gasped in horror.

"What's wrong, Alec?", I asked, thinking he may have seen a snake close by. But no, he was pointing down the grassy slope. A long way into the distance I saw about a dozen Africans armed with what looked like machetes. They were far away but were intently heading for us.

"Don't worry, Alec. We will have the spare wheel on before they can reach us."

"But you don't understand, Cy. The jack is a bit dodgy."

It was now my turn to inherit a concerned look on my face. If Paddy had said this I would have been tempted to believe he was joking. But, no, not Alec, not a ghost of a chance. It must be so. Alec seemed fascinated, with his eyes staring at the distant threat.

I started winding the jack, determined that we would get the job done. The jack seemed okay. The chassis was rising very slowly when suddenly, it dropped down two notches. I commenced again, carefully winding it slowly, making steady progress, when once again, it dropped down. 'This is getting serious', I thought. Keeping calm in these situations is most beneficial and it had me in good stead on previous occasions.

Alec was giving me a yard by yard commentary on the progress of this band of Mau Mau, punctuated with, "I knew we should not have come, we'll both be hacked to death". This utterance of his (and especially the last line) did wonders for me, as you might guess. Reminding me that it could be a possibility, if not, a probability.

I was winning the battle with the jack. Four up, then a drop back of two or three. It was taking a laboriously long time and was quite soul-destroying. My only pessimistic thought (a miserable one), was the consequence of this wretched jack dropping right down to zero or even halfway.

Alec was almost jumping up and down by now, so I assumed that they must be getting closer. I was squatting by the jack with my back towards them when I came to a decision. I was not concerned about winding any more, because previous to the last wind-up it had dropped down three ratchets. It was holding now, and the thought of it dropping down three more ratchets was quite frightening. The wheel was barely off the ground and I knew that the inflated spare wheel would need a bit more space to fit it on the hub, yet I took the existing wheel off the studs.

"Quick," I shouted at Alec in a commanding voice. "Line the spare wheel up to the wheel studs and when I say, 'Push!', push the wheel on as hard as you can." Then, bracing myself, legs apart, I lifted the bodywork up the last inch. Thank goodness it's wasn't a big Mercedes.

"Now!", I shouted. Alec pushed, and on went the wheel. I've never tightened wheel nuts so fast. "Start her up", I said, and for the first time I looked around and saw that they were almost upon us. I kicked the cursed jack away and jumped in. We moved quickly away throwing up loads of shale, praying he didn't stall the car in the desperate act of escaping. I could not and did not look back. All the way to Thika Alec was muttering, "I knew we shouldn't have come. I shouldn't have let you talk me into it!".

I thought inwardly that he had a valid point, and tended to half-heartedly agree with him. Even though he was gripping the steering wheel I could see that he was visibly shaking. Poor Sod!

He started shouting, "We almost got murdered back there! I'll have nightmares for the rest of my life about being hacked to death! I've not stopped shaking! And once again, we shouldn't have come!". Then he turned his tortured face towards me and said, "Why don't you say something?".

"You haven't paused for breath, Alec. How could I? I agree. It was a very near thing." Then, with tongue in cheek, "But it was very exciting, wasn't it? Better than sitting about in Nairobi". I knew instantly that it was a very insensitive thing to say to him, and a little too flippant in the light of what had just happened. It was just bravado on my part! He looked at me in utter disbelief. He was dumbfounded! Hoping to joke my way out of it and unwind him in the process I said, "Just think, Alec. You will be able to tell your grandchildren all about the narrow escape you had today. Try to put it out of your mind and as a distraction think of all those lovely cakes we are going to have in Thika!". I thought he was going to be sick!! Secretly, I could have done justice to a bucketful of brandy. I hadn't the nerve, or such lack of compassion, to remind him that we had the return journey to do — without a jack.

We reported the incident to the local police post in Thika and then went on to the café. It was a nice place. It was rather large, colonial in style and contained a surprising number of people milling around inside. A very motherly, buxom lady in a nice clean floral 'pinny', greeted us with a beaming smile from behind a table laden with a great variety of the most delicious cakes.

Justice was duly done to the fayre laid out in front of us. Even Alec tucked in with a wan smile in my direction, probably gaining confidence now that safety was assured with so many fellow beings around him. Tea was served in a proper, nice, china teapot. Not the usual pewter ones, which seemed so popular. Our progress through the cake display was observed with amusement by those around us. It seemed to be a popular place, and most probably a Sunday ritual for the local community who seemed so blasé about such a table of goodies.

The local characters, I surmised, were mostly white Kenya settlers. The majority were middle-aged and optimistic in their outlook. A group of them in our vicinity were quite interested and concerned as we relayed to them the incident we had been involved in. One gentleman had a large handlebar moustache, was red and round of face and dressed in khaki jodhpurs. He was albeit a retired Indian Colonel type and said in a suitably booming voice, "There is a party of us going into Nairobi late this afternoon, in two Land Rovers. If you care to accompany us in your car, you will be very welcome". It was just the tonic required to bring Alec out of his worried state. He positively beamed at me when hearing this wonderful offer!! We both expressed our thanks on acceptance.

We had an uneventful return to Nairobi. It was quite an anti-climax. On our journey back, near the site of the breakdown, I received an expected, firm negative answer from Alec (who was looking straight ahead as though on a mission to outer space), when I suggested we stop and look for the abandoned jack.

He was so relieved, and even turned and smiled at me, as we entered Nairobi. On arriving at the Queen's he said to me, "If you want to go on any more trips, you can go on your own. Don't expect me to pander to your ego. I wish to live a lot longer and enjoy my life". And with that, he went up the stairs to the room. He didn't answer me when I called to him, "Not one for the road then, Alec?". Then realising the significance of the word 'road' and thinking 'miserable sod', I headed through to the bar and wondered if any other guest had ever given serious thought to ordering a bucket of brandy.

CHAPTER 3

After we had arrived back in Nairobi from our Thika adventure, Alec had plenty of extra work to deal with. Most days he arrived back at the hotel quite late and seemed to be a little reluctant to become involved in any evening activities. I think our recent escapade may have had a bearing on this. As a result, I sat alone in the hotel lounge in the evening.

After a few evenings, I became increasingly aware that I was a source of interest for two young ladies who were giving deft, yet obvious glances and half-smiles in my direction. Sometimes a middle-aged lady was present with them, and consequently, their interest was muted. They appeared to rebuff any other male interest even when 'Mama', the other lady, was not with them. So why the interest in me? Not averse to female company, I naturally welcomed and encouraged them.

I had inherited a high degree of chivalry from my father (it must be in the genes), who was also completely at ease in the company of the fairer sex. He was a courageous man who had borne illness throughout most of his life without complaint or self-pity and yet had a natural twinkle in his eyes, accompanied with an engaging personality. He brought me up on a strict 'manners maketh man' diet with a natural impressionable emphasis towards the ladies. Naturally, one evening when the mutual interest was obviously well advanced, I went across to their table and asked permission to join them. They seemed very pleased and it was all smiles as I sat down.

During the evening they asked me if I would join them for dinner with their employer, 'The Boss'. They were working for a private firm in Nairobi and wished to impress their boss with the type of company they were keeping. Plus, they were encouraged by the fact that it would make a balanced party. I had mixed feelings of flattery, or perhaps being used for their own ends but who cares? They seemed like nice characters.

The two girls had known each other for quite some time, were good friends, and very good company. The fact that there weren't many talented young ladies around, or any other interesting company, decided me to play along with them. They were, I guessed, in their mid-twenties.

Anne was a small, auburn-haired girl, who had lived in Kenya with her parents for many years and was well educated. Her father had died and she now stayed at the hotel as a resident with her mother, who led her own life but did accompany Anne on occasions. So, this was the middle-aged lady I had seen previously.

Jodi was the name of the other girl. She was about five foot six inches tall, with dark hair. Born in Switzerland she had an occasional, very slight accent that was complemented with a very attractive low, slightly husky voice. She had her own room at the hotel. They were attractive, both in appearance and in their different personalities.

I got on well with their boss over dinner and held court a few times on certain subjects, which impressed the girls and added to the evening's success. I was really looking forward to our evenings in the lounge, now. We had many laughs and the three of us were good company for each other. Gradually, I could sense an increasing attraction from both the girls, which was reciprocated.

One evening, Anne was quite serious when she warned me of being too familiar with the African hotel staff. I couldn't see any reason why I should not be friendly, especially to my breakfast waiter, Dongu. He was a tall figure with a nice character. He was always pleased to see me and would greet me with a smile, position my chair for me and always supplied me with two eggs and other extras. In my book, I considered him friendly and I showed it. Anne was insistent and sincere. I remember her holding my arm, leaning quite close to me, her resolute little face so attractive, especially being so close.

Earnestly she said, "The Mau Mau element gain popularity by convincing the African population that they are being downtrodden by the white people. You might think you are gaining brownie points with the Africans, but there are, I should imagine, quite a few hotel staff with Mau Mau sympathies, if not actively involved. You could possibly be a target for them because you are going against what the Mau Mau are teaching".

I thanked her for the warning, appreciating the fact that she knew much more about Kenyans and their customs than I did, being a mere novice in the country. 'What a turn up for the books!', as the saying goes. Causing a person to become your enemy by being friendly to them is not normally logical but could be so, after understanding and appreciating Anne's warning.

It shook me to the core and I was taken aback in utter disbelief when Dongu was arrested as a major figure in a Mau Mau gang. I thought Anne was very sweet when we heard the news. It was not a case of triumph, or 'I told you so'. There was no exhilaration of the fact that she had been proven right. No, just a lovely smile as she squeezed my arm, and with her face once again very close, said, "I would hate to lose you!". I noticed a distinct twinkle in her eyes!

Some time later I was negotiating the stairs during the day when I met Jodi. She stopped me and asked if I could repair her iron which had suddenly stopped functioning. I said, "Certainly I will. When would you like me to call?".

"Is it possible this evening because I am lost without it, and I have a few things to press?"

I agreed and called at her room early in the evening. I knocked at her door and heard, "Come in".

Upon entering the room I saw she was sitting up in bed. She said that she had gone to bed suffering from a headache. Various thoughts on the feasibility of Jodi's reason started running through and around inside my head. Should I believe it? Should I attempt to join her? But on checking the iron I found it was indeed faulty and in a dangerous condition. I managed to re-terminate and repair the flex, for which she was truly grateful. She gave me no obvious sign that she wished me to join her, so I said, "Trust you will be feeling better by the morning, Jodi" and left her.

Outside I was at sixes and sevens. She did say that she had a headache, and the iron was truly faulty. If I had made any advances towards her in those circumstances, it could have been a terrible faux pas and probably the loss of my friendship with her. Yet, on the other hand, she might think me a terribly naïve, cold-blooded Englander. I opted for my original decision because I would not have wished to lose my friendship with Jodi, and possibly, with Anne (which was more important to me than the loss of face). But I still thought of her bed. A nice good romp there would have done me the world of good, I'm sure. And probably Jodi, too!

Anne was away that evening with her mother and I wondered if this was opportunism on Jodi's part? Or was it just coincidental? Mmm! I was somewhat restless that night in bed, thinking about what might have been.

I couldn't believe it when two evenings later before dinner, I met Anne also on the stairs! Was this another contrived meeting? She told me that Jodi would not be joining us that evening and asked if I would like a change of scene by accompanying her to a small hotel on the outskirts of Nairobi for a drink after dinner. I agreed with alacrity! Oh yes definitely, I thought. A change of scene? Another coincidence? Jodi absent?! It sounded like it could be a very interesting evening! At least Anne didn't have a headache!

We duly left in her car, after dinner. This was more like it, something different. She certainly knew her way around Nairobi and being Kenya born was very confident in the way that she conducted herself, drove, and was so fluent in her conversations with the Africans.

We eventually arrived at the Countryside Hotel and had a lovely evening chatting about her life. She listened to the description of my life in England and we finished a very pleasant evening nice and relaxed.

"I'll take you back a different way, for a change", she said, as we drove away from the hotel.

We were travelling along a quiet out-of-town road when she suddenly pulled into a small clearing by the side of the road.

"I've not run out of petrol, Cy," she said, as she stopped the car. "I've stopped so that I can do something I have wanted to do for some time." With that remark, she leant across and kissed me quickly. I thought it a splendid idea and quickly shuffled nearer to her. She immediately came back at me and we had a most prolonged, deeply intensive kiss. Her left hand was on the back of my seat to support herself and her other hand had landed on my left thigh. During our prolonged kiss she kept it moving and twitching, which was having a most intense effect upon me.

She then withdrew and suggested that we move into the rear seat. Such an amicable suggestion to which I readily agreed. Whilst we were moving there I made sure that all the doors were locked and although Anne assured me that it was a safe area, agreed it was wise to lock up.

We both realised the attraction and need for each other. The first kiss was the striking of the match and the second meaningful kiss was the lighting of the fire. The fire raged as we both realised what we were missing and what had imperceptibly grown in the last few weeks of knowing each other.

When the fire had eventually run its course, a deep feeling of utter bliss encompassed me. Anne was lying limp and partially slumped in the corner of the rear seat. The expression on her face resembled the cat who had just finished the cream. We took stock of ourselves. Our clothes were outrageously disarranged and scattered. Her panties were hanging from one of her toes, and goodness knows where her shoes were! The windows were all steamed up in a very obvious way. She gazed at me with a sort of glazed look and I must have looked the same.

She croaked, "It's a good job we didn't realise our need for each other in the middle of Nairobi, Cy!! The car rocking the way it was could have raised some eyebrows!!". This symbolised Anne. I loved her sense of humour and thought, 'I could really love this girl'. It seemed all the funnier, her uttering this witticism, lying there whacked out and showing everything to the world.

To me, Anne was an ideal companion. She faced the world with her chin up, like me. Not only were we great lovers and so good for each other she was also so easy to converse with and had a good and sometimes wicked sense of humour. Once, when the opportunity presented itself in the hotel lounge, she sidled up to me and whispered, "I'm due for a service, and could really do with one. How about you?".

One day, after we had made love and were just having a cuddle, she said, "Jodi would be terribly upset and even jealous if she knew what we get up to".

"She doesn't know yet? Hasn't she guessed?"

"No," said Anne, "Jodi told me that she lured you into her bedroom one evening when I was out somewhere, on the pretext to mend her iron. The iron was one that had not been used for a long time because it had been faulty. She said that she got into her bed, ready and in the mood for you, but all you did was repair the iron and left!! Just like a gentleman.

Jodi supposed she shouldn't have expected you to fancy her and wondered if you aren't inclined that way! She also said that she still values you as a friend, and who knows, perhaps, one day things may change!!"

The modern quotation, 'Men are from Mars and women are from Venus' would surely have echoed my sentiments if it had been known then! Why have they to be so devious? Why mention a headache? It's the last word a man wants to hear!! Anne was giggling, which was very infectious!

"That's made you think, Cy! You will just have to accept the fact that she was the one that got away! I'm only mentioning this now, love, because it looks like Jodi will be returning to Switzerland. She had a letter today to say that her mother is very ill. I can't see her returning to Kenya because I know that she is more than happy to return to nurse her mother, and to take part in running the family business."

What a situation. How fate can be decided! What if Jodi had not mentioned her headache? What if? Yes, it is often 'what if?' that can decide the future! Who knows? I might have become quite involved in a cuckoo clock business in Switzerland. Now my main consideration was Anne. I was completely besotted with her. As I mentioned earlier, her giggling was infectious and was genuine. I loved the broad mind she had and the happiness surrounding her.

When we next met, Jodi confirmed that she would be returning home in a fortnight, which would give her time to clear her commitments in Nairobi. I said that I would be sorry to see her go and that I would miss her.

A few days later I noticed that Anne seemed somewhat subdued and quieter than normal. She said she was okay, so I presumed that it was the thought of losing her friend. She seemed very reluctant to let go of me, holding my sleeve on occasions, and clingy (I think describes it) when it wasn't even a passionate moment. Sometimes I caught her with her eyes full of tears, then she would be herself again. Hormones? A woman's biological difference, I knew, could play havoc with their emotions, but she assured me that she wasn't ill.

When the time came for Jodi to return home it was arranged that Anne would drive her to the airport. I said goodbye to her the evening before she left due to work commitments the next day. When Anne was away from us for a little while Jodi said, "I'm sorry to have to leave you, Cy. Anne has told me about your relationship with her. I, too, would have loved to have known you better but it was not to be. I think Anne has something to tell you but is finding it hard to do so. She has been worried about it for a few days now".

"What is it about, Jodi. Do you know?"

"Yes, I know, Cy. But Anne will have to tell. I can't." With that last remark, Anne joined us.

That night as I lay in bed, I thought perhaps it might be because she is pregnant!! She is going to have a baby despite telling me that there would be no problem and that she had that aspect under control. Still, mistakes and accidents can happen!! It can't be anything else!! Well, that's okay with me. I'll propose to her if that is the case. I could think of nothing better than sharing my life with such a splendid girl, plus a baby as a bonus. I laid awake most of the night but when I awoke the next morning I felt strangely elated.

Two evenings later when we were out together on our own again, I put both hands gently under her chin, looked into her eyes and said, "If we are having a baby, you can bet your life that I will be the happiest man on this earth and I would love to spend my life with you". I saw the tears well up into her eyes and roll down her cheeks and could feel her whole body shudder. Then she started sobbing. I thought that this might be because of my reaction to her pregnancy and that it was a loving, tearful release from her worry. But, no!! Her sobbing intensified and I just took hold of her, holding her close.

Then, between the sobs she blurted out, "I love you so much, Cy. I really do. I'd love to spend my life with you too but I know you will never forgive me. You will hate me now!! Hate me!!". She was saying it with quite some venom. "I've let you down. How could I be so cruel to you? So cruel to someone I love and hold so dear." Then, her tearful, wet, beautiful little face looked up at me and said in a faint trembling voice, "I'm not pregnant, darling, and I can't marry you at present, because I am already married!!". She continued, her voice hardly audible, "I had a letter from my husband a few days ago!!".

Speechless and shocked in utter disbelief, I tried to grapple with my emotions. It can't be true. It must be a bad dream!! Now her tears cascaded. Although I felt stunned and absolutely wretched, I couldn't bear to see her in this state and so dreadfully unhappy. I said, "Okay, pet. You will feel better now that you have got it off your mind. It must be a big release for you and it has not altered my love for you. You still stand six feet tall as always, I can hardly reach you". She laughed and gulped air between sobs. I was always joking about our different heights.

After much reassurances and convincing her repeatedly that I didn't hate her, her body gradually relaxed and seemed almost limp. I said, "When you feel a little better and are brave enough to face the world, we will go back to the hotel and have a drink. You can tell me all about it, the letter from your husband etc.".

"Oh yes, I will do that, Cy. I can't believe you are not angry with me. I was dreading the thought of you just leaving me in disgust, abruptly, and very angry. The thought of you leaving me like that filled me with dread and it was that thought that had made me feel so wretched and unhappy."

We returned to the hotel where she freshened up and came back into the lounge. She looked much better but was still a little puffy around her eyes. She sat down and looked at me with love and determination. God, how I loved this girl! I reached across the table, squeezed her hand and smiled to give her confidence. After a short interval of inspecting the table, she looked up.

"About eighteen months ago my husband, John, volunteered for a post upcountry to work on a coffee plantation. He knew full well that it was the last place I wanted us to be, but he couldn't refuse the salary and the other perks. He promised that he could save enough for us to live in Mombasa, where I have always wanted to be. He hardly kept in touch, saying that he was working and saving for our future. I thought my marriage must be on the decline and that he must be interested elsewhere.

"When you arrived in the hotel lounge both Jodi and I were interested to see how you would cope because it was obvious to us that you were fresh from the UK. Of course, being two girls in the lounge we attracted the interest of male residents, but we declined their invitations. Jodi, because she classed them all as 'lounge lizards' and out for all they could get, and I because I was married! We were amused to see how you coped with ordering a drink. Not only ordering, but we knew the effect the altitude would have on you because we had seen it all before, and we weren't disappointed. Both of us agreed you managed the stairs better than most and so you became our interest. Although Jodi and I are very good friends, the evening could be a bit boring.

"Our interest rose when you stood at the bar one evening with a group of lizards. They all seemed slouched and yet you were erect in your stature. Jodi was very impressed by your courtesy when a lady with two or three companions joined you for a short while at your table. 'There's class for you,' said Jodi, 'I wouldn't mind a slice of that. I quite fancy him, Anne. He's doing very well seeing that he's only just come on board'.

"I hadn't realised my feelings until Jodi passed that remark. I felt a pang of jealousy. 'Me too. I wouldn't mind either!', I said. 'It would be great if we could capture him in time for Walter's evening dinner to see what makes him tick.' So, we were thrilled when you came across and introduced yourself just in time to invite you to the dinner!

"As the days went by you became the most important topic, especially for Jodi. When we heard of your Thika escapade, the thought of you being hacked to death made us shudder and I thought to myself, 'This man needs protection from himself and if he wants excitement, Jodi could well do that! And if Jodi couldn't then I most certainly could!'. The other concern was my mother. If you two met she might spill the beans so I had to juggle to keep you both apart. When Jodi told me about the bedroom incident, I was surprised".

"Stop a moment, Anne", I said, "Jodi told me that she had a headache".

"All the more reason to have tried to make it better", replied Anne. "How otherwise could she have explained why she was in bed?" Shaking her head she said, "Men!".

"Complicated women", I said.

She was beginning to look like herself again now and was smiling. She continued, "I was intrigued and thought, 'Surely we are not reading him that wrong, although he hasn't made advances on either of us. It was then that I decided to take a hand and invite you out. Well, I had to try!

"After a drink to give me a little more courage, I stopped the car. I was really worked up and aroused, anticipating and visualising the moments. I don't know how I would have coped if you had proved Jodi right and been uninterested in women. Wow! You know the rest, Cy.

"I was so wrapped up in you and the promise of our future until suddenly I had this letter from John. He said that he was finishing upcountry and had secured employment in Mombasa. He couldn't wait for us to get back together and said that all the separation would be worthwhile."

"What is John like? If you decide to leave him, how do you think he will take it?"

Her brow furrowed as she thought for a moment then reluctantly said, "Badly. I will be honest, Cy, I think he will be devastated. But with my feelings for you, I would be prepared to be selfish for our happiness together".

It was getting late now as we both realised with a start. I said, "It's off your chest now, if not from your mind, pet. I don't think either of us will sleep properly tonight but given a bit of time, we will sort it out together".

So, back to the Queen's we went. I did not sleep very well, as you might imagine and I must have looked haggard when I met Anne at lunchtime the next day. She said, "I've told Mum everything and she wants to meet you!!".

I felt my eyebrows shoot up. "Was she annoyed?"

"No," Anne replied. "She called me a fool for not trusting or confiding in her. She said she would have been happy to make other arrangements for herself so that you could have had her share of the room."

Anne then said that she thought her Mum needed an excuse to move in with her male companion but didn't want her daughter to be left on her own. I thought to myself of all the time we could have spent together. Ah well!!

I met her Mum that evening in the hotel lounge. As Anne introduced me to her, her mother smiled at me and said, "Oh!! You're the one? I thought as much. I often saw you looking over at our table and wondered which of the girls you were interested in. I knew it couldn't be me! I thought it might be Jodi, her being single but I was wrong. So we have some sorting to do, haven't we?".

Her Mum struck me as a very practical lady. I could see Anne in her. She was approximately the same size as Anne but a bit more rounded and bigger bosomed. More a motherly figure. She oozed personality with a disarming friendly smile and was very self-assured and confident. I liked her, just like all the Kenya characters I had met. She pointed out that no matter how much in love we were it would be very difficult in the short and long term to stay together and our future happiness could well be jeopardised. Although Anne and I had had time for our emotions to stabilise a little, it was still difficult to keep them under control whilst discussions continued with her Mum.

Her Mum continued, "Just think about it, Cy. Any posting that you might be given would be based on a single person accommodation because in the eyes of your administration you are single. Plus, because your administration covers Kenya, Tanganyika, and Uganda it could be anywhere in the three territories, and in unknown circumstances".

To Anne, she said, "You were not unhappy with John were you, Anne?". Anne agreed very reluctantly. "It's not as though you hate John. It would be devastating for him and I don't know whether he could cope with it. Knowing both of you — I know it is only briefly, Cy, but I judge you to be an honourable man — I don't think you could live happily together, basing your life on someone else's sorrow and misery.

"I do advise that you view this part of your life as a whole episode, much enjoyed and valued along life's long highway. What I suggest now is for you to enjoy life to the full, until you, Anne, have to move to Mombasa in a fortnight. I will move out of the room and Cy, you must try and get the next fortnight off. Anne, you go and see Walter. Tell him from me (as a close friend of his), that you have to resign. And ask if he could absolve you from working your notice. Both of you must think it over and then decide what you wish to do."

Noticing my quizzical look, her Mum said, "Don't worry about the morals of the situation, Cy. It is said, 'Are you married or do you live in Kenya?'. Well, we might as well live up to it!".

Why not? I thought 'What a wonderful woman', and I told her so. I also thanked her for her wisdom, advice, help and understanding. We both gave her a big hug before we left and went to our beds to mull things over once again.

I met Anne the following afternoon. She had been helping her Mum to move out of the room. She had also seen Walter who readily agreed to Anne's request. Not only did he grant her immediate leave but would pay her as well! I began to wonder how friendly Anne's Mum and Walter really were! He also sent his best wishes to me. I had thought he was a nice character from the dinner we spent together and this confirmed my opinion of him.

We made arrangements with the hotel management and changed rooms. Alec wished me all the best and seemed concerned as to who he might get as a roommate.

In my new room, Anne and I discussed the situation and accepted that there was a mountain to climb. Not just the practicalities but also our emotions and the possible emotions of John, depending on our decision. I was feeling increasingly sorry for John. He was being discussed with someone else deciding the future for him! There was also the concern of my future postings and whether the admin would treat me as a single person. So many anomalies were discussed as we both talked so easily together deep into the night, so compatible were we, cuddled up in bed. We decided to remain in her bed and eventually, emotionally exhausted, with my protective arm around her we dropped off to sleep.

The next morning, we showered, dressed and went down to breakfast. It seemed strange to sit at a different table and wave to Alec at my original table. Anne and I sat opposite each other by mutual agreement. That way we would both be in each other's sight.

After exploring every avenue and both being honest and caring people, we came to a very reluctant decision to accept Mum's advice. Anything else, we believed, could well turn out to be disastrous for all concerned. We really would be haunted by basing our future on someone else's sorrow and misery. Although it would and did feel, that a death sentence was hanging over us, we decided to enjoy what time we had left together.

Being in transition with my next posting unconfirmed, I did not foresee any difficulty in getting the fortnight off and expected to merely forfeit leave sometime later in the year. The next morning I applied for the two weeks leave, and it was granted. I had also heard about a scheme whereupon the administration grants an interest-free loan to purchase a car. On enquiring about this generous offer I was informed that it only came into force after being resident in the country for six months. The privilege of driving Anne around was denied to me.

The car that Anne had been using was in fact, her Mum's Chevrolet. There were quite a few on the streets of Nairobi. "Keep it for the fortnight", her Mum had told her. Such a lovely Mum, such a lovely daughter and such a lovely relationship!!

There was no stopping Anne now. "I'll show you Kenya, Cy! We will go to the Game Parks, Nairobi National Park and the Ngorongoro Crater in Tanganyika (which is about one hundred and fifty miles south). You'll love it, I know you will."

Early one morning, both dressed in shorts and shirts (she looked superb) we journeyed forth out on to the Mombasa road. The sun came up so quickly, like a huge orange, inviting us into another day. We turned off at Athi River and headed on through Kajiado towards Kilimanjaro, which stood majestically in the distance. The road looked dusty and sandy, yet the murram dust had compacted into hard corrugations, which typifies the out-of-town roads in East Africa. It gave us a bumpy ride when travelling below 40 mph. The faster we went, the smoother the ride. We were floating on top of the ridges, so to speak. Massive dust clouds billowed out behind us we passed through Namanga and Longido.

We eventually arrived at Arusha (which is in Tanzania now) by the side of Mount Meru, which is nestled like a smaller sister near to her big brother, Mount Kilimanjaro. We did discuss the possibility of climbing the mountain instead of going on towards the Serengeti but decided against it. Although it was a feasible (but hard) climb, there was such a lot of cloud around the mountain. Secondly, the Ngorongoro Crater and the vast surrounding country with it's associated animal life beckoned. So, off we went, down to Makuyuni just like two happy bunnies passing Lake Manyara on our left.

We saw so many elephants, the elusive leopard, a cheetah and her cubs, all the different types of gazelle, wildebeest, just about everything. Anne, being born in this lovely country, knew the rules. She seemed to know, or sense, the locations. One of her uncles, I think she said, was a big game hunter, who used to take 'the rich few' around the areas.

The highlight of all these days was when we stopped in a clearing with a pride of lionesses just lazing in the sun and shade. The cubs climbing and enjoying life, just like domestic kittens do. Then up came 'The Bwana', the lion himself. He came so close, sat down and leaned on the side of the car near the left side rear wheel. I was rightly concerned, but Anne said, "Don't worry, Cy. They don't see us as a threat. The car fuel masks our body scent. If you are ever threatened by a lion, never try to stare them out. Look slightly to the side of them, keeping them in sight, like any other cat would do if they aren't seeking confrontation. That way, you are not promoting a challenge". That advice stood me in good stead many moons later, and proved to be vital!

We spent such lovely days together, drinking in the beauty and excitements of this lovely country, experiencing the Masai greetings, making love in unique situations, seemingly drinking the expensive wine of life — so utterly lost to everything. The most important thing that mattered was being one with one other.

Utter despair brewed as the terrible day dawned. Mum came and drove us to the station. On the platform, a great big Garratt locomotive, hissed at all and sundry, waiting like the devil to take my loved one from me! Mum hugged Anne and said some quiet words to her. After saying her goodbye she stood aside. Anne, now close to me, turned her brave little face up towards mine and we just held each other until the whistle went. We had both said previously that we would be very brave at parting and Anne had promised that only if her marital situation changed, would she get in touch with me, via my administration.

No one could say that we weren't brave but as we parted, tears were running down her cheeks. Being a 'control freak', I hate to admit it, I couldn't control mine either. With a terrible lump in my throat and tears trickling down our cheeks, we tried to laugh and be brave. I waved until the sight of her was lost. Then I turned around into her Mum's arms and noticed her eyes were full of tears too. Yes! The emotion had got to this very practical woman also. Then I heard her say, "Come on, Cy. You are a good man, I'll buy you a drink!". What a lovely Mum!

CHAPTER 4

As you can well imagine I was dejected after Anne had left and could not face the Queen's lounge or the dining room. Without my beloved Anne, I hated both places and decided immediately to leave the hotel. I saw Ron, the manager, whom I was getting to know quite well, to tell him of my intentions. Surprisingly he seemed to be expecting me and ushered me into his office.

I came straight to the point with: "I'm sorry, Ron but I must leave your hotel and find other accommodation".

Immediately he cut in: "I understand your position. Cy! —".

"How the hell do you think that you know my position?!" I suspected that I must have come across a little arrogant. Obviously, the way I was feeling bore the responsibility for that attitude.

"First of all, I make it my business to know what is going on in my hotel. And secondly, I know and have known Anne, and especially her mum for many years. Anne's mum told me that she thought you would be visiting me!"

I couldn't believe it! It seemed like a social club with these Kenya types. Who the hell did Anne's mum not know? I wondered what they had discussed and come up with now!

He said, "Your administration, plus some private firms have contracts with me to accommodate their staff. To move from the hotel you would first obtain their agreement. I do sympathise with you, Cy, and have come up with a solution. Anne's mum thinks it is a good idea too".

I thought to myself that I would have to get used to how things are decided and sorted here in Kenya and hoped that one day I would gradually become less bemused. Everything about Anne and I had been 'sorted' but now it was even my accommodation which seemed to have been thoroughly discussed. It was so comical and so simple, people chatting and sorting things out for others. If I hadn't felt so tragic I would have been amused.

"We have a hotel annexe on the edge of Nairobi with a few rooms. At the moment there are two family rooms and three singles and I have just one single vacant. You could move in there if you so desire and eat here in the grill room attached to the hotel. Most items from the hotel menu that you are familiar with are served there." He shook me when he said, "In fact, your ex-roommate, Mr Horton moved to the annexe the other evening".

Incredulously I said, "Alec? Why was that? What made him move there?".

"His firm also has a contract with us and Mr Horton wanted a single room. He was not happy with the person he was sharing with and complained that he snored heavily and was uncouth."

That decided me! Alec, oh yes dear old Alec, with his transport there and back!!

"Oh yes, Ron, I will take up your offer. I do accept and thank you, especially for your understanding. Please give my love and thanks to Anne's Mum." I felt like adding another success for the 'committee' but refrained from doing so. I mused about Alec's decision. Dear, dear old Alec! I felt a teeny bit better all of a sudden!

I arrived at the annexe and surprised Alec leaving his room. Initially, he looked a picture of apprehension and puzzlement, plus a hint of disbelief. When I explained my situation to him he seemed somewhat relieved and welcomed my presence.

"I'm glad you have come to stay here, Cy. I'm sorry I came here since it is very vulnerable to Mau Mau attacks, especially being so isolated."

I stopped him with: "We are not far from the main road Alec. Don't worry so much. It's lovely and quiet. So peaceful".

"So quiet? Yes, it is. Especially when the children have gone to bed. But I don't like it at all. There are no outside lights." Pointing to the bushes he said, "They could quite easily conceal someone!".

"How many people are staying here, Alec?"

"Well, there is Mavis and William in No. 1 with their children. In No. 2 is a married couple. I think their names are Bert and Helen? Then room No. 3 is Roy Smith on his own. He's out at the moment."

"How old are they at a guess?"

"Oh, all about thirty to fortyish", he said.

"So, we have five able-bodied blokes around. Well that's not too bad, is it?"

At this point in our conversation, Roy Smith came in to view. Alec introduced us and then continued out to wherever he was going. Roy and I started the process of getting to know each other. We immediately hit it off. "God it's boring here," he said. "Alec doesn't seem to spark at all."

"Well, I'm just moving in."

"Oh good, I guessed you might be. I've been here for some time now. Come on in, I'm in No. 3. Let's have a drink, I've got the odd bottle."

I took stock of Roy. He was the same build and weight as me but with dark hair somewhat brushed back. He was from the UK, near the London area (I guessed). He was relaxed, smiling and pretty sure of himself. I liked him!!

"Fancy going out on the town tonight, Cy? Alec won't go out after dark. It's a damn good walk into Nairobi, but it's worth it, except for being a bit of a pig on one's own."

"Brilliant! I'll put my things away, have a shower and we'll go." I saw his eyes light up and we both grinned at each other. What a tonic for me after all the heartbreak and trauma. This will help — good medicine!

We walked fast into town. Thank God he walked fast, I can't stand shuffling along. We passed the Queen's and headed for the Chez De, a reasonably select night club. It was situated on the first floor, beautifully furnished and had a most extravagant bar.

We ordered a drink. It was quiet, being too early in the evening for the night club. Yet, earlier when we were passing the Queen's there seemed to be a dance or something going on.

"It's a bit early in the evening to be in here, Roy. Don't you think?" Then I realised his attention was elsewhere. I followed his gaze to two tall, graceful, dark-haired ladies with Grecian complexions. One of whom was smiling at him.

"Come on, Cy. Let's see if we can buy them a drink."

I reluctantly went over with him. Reluctant because Anne had not left my thoughts. I had not the slightest interest. Roy had only just started a few pleasantries with them when two well-built, mafia-style men in dark, expensive suits came through the doors. It was obvious by the olive colour of their skin who they had come to see.

A stand-off situation developed immediately. The two girls suddenly lost their friendly smiles and developed wooden countenances. We moved away from the girls just to let the men know that we had read the situation. One of them moved his hand towards what could be a shoulder holster. As he did so 'Smithy' (Roy) did the same. Tit for tat, the man withdrew his empty hand. We both moved away from them towards the door leaving them the 'field' because it wasn't our scene anyway.

They seemed to relax when they saw that we were leaving. The nearest to me actually smiled, probably because a confrontation had been averted and they realised that we were not after their women.

We were three-quarters of the way down the stairs when the door from the club burst open and both men came through shouting profanities (I presume) in a foreign tongue. They launched themselves down the stairs. One had a gun in his hand and the other was fumbling for his. I shouted, "Roy your gun!".

"I haven't got a bloody gun!"

"Jeez!! Leg it rapidly", I said. And we did.

They pursued us out of the door but although they were big, muscular men and tougher than both of us, I don't think they were as fit. We dodged around some metal dustbins on the corner and then ducked into the side road to avoid them having a long field of fire, thence into the back roads of Nairobi. This tactic was a bit dodgy because so many odd characters inhabited the backstreets. It was a dimly lit area where a pungent smell of food flavoured with charcoal smoke filled the air. We seemed to have caught the local inhabitants by surprise, running through their so-called territory. Walking of course would have been a foolhardy and dangerous thing to do.

Running was no picnic either. Robbery would not have been the only probability. "We'll head up towards the other side road in the direction of the Queen's, Roy", I shouted between lungfuls of air. Just as I finished speaking a bullet hit the side wall of a small dwelling just to the left of us. I was not amused. I thought, 'Sod this for a game of soldiers, this is serious stuff!!'. Why were the men so fired up? They seemed quite okay when we left. Had the girls said something? Why had they changed their minds? The questions were running through my confused brain.

Then, Roy almost fell over a bundle of rags. I thought he was going to fall but for what seemed like an age of trying to keep on his feet he managed to stay upright. He delivered a mouthful of obscenities through gasps. I almost did the same thing trying to miss an iron cooking pot. Another bullet hit the wall not very far from Roy but I thought it must be a desperate attempt on their part because we seemed to be outstripping them now. Still, it only needed one bullet to be on target.

God, I felt we had been running for miles. Roy gasped, "Up this alley, Cy. Let's chance it". I thought to myself 'Yes, it could cut a corner off and I'm sure is in the right direction'. The danger of taking this chance was having to run in single file in the confines of the alley, thus presenting them with an easier target. I went first, with the alley being on my side. In the dimly lit confines I had to watch for drunken bodies and debris strewn about yet pushing our speed to the utmost. We hoped that because the alley was not too long we could turn onto the road before they could reach the beginning of the alley. We managed to achieve this and both grunted as we recognised that it was the backroad leading up to the Queen's. Hopefully we could get there before they emerged from the alley and consequently lose them.

Up the road, we went crossing over to the other side and into the Queen's through the side door. I should imagine they might guess that we had gone into the Queen's but they would not be sure.

A dance was in full swing and we lost ourselves immediately in the crowd, causing stares and raised eyebrows at our almost bent figures, gasping for breath. We straightened up a little but were still breathing heavily, if not gasping when I suddenly came face to face with Ron. I saw the two pursuers scanning the room through the windows of the hotel.

Ron had followed my eyes, (he did not miss much) and seemed amused. "You certainly tend to court disaster don't you, Cy?" Then, in a lowered voice he said, "They won't come in here". Returning to his natural voice and eyeing Roy he said, "You have a somewhat peculiar choice of dancing partner and I know you have not got an invitation to this private party. I suppose you will have to be my guest. Come on I'll buy you both a drink. God knows you look as though you need one!".

We moved further away from the actual dancing and sat down with our drinks. I noticed that Roy's cheek was denoted with dried blood. It was a mystery as to where he got the cut from.

After relaxing for a minute or two Roy said, "Quite an evening!".

"Mmm," I said, "It certainly was. It puzzles me as to why they changed their minds and transformed into such a killer mood!".

Roy paused a little. I sensed he was holding something back. "Well… I think it must have been this 'honour' thing that these foreigners have."

"What honour thing?", I said.

"I think we dishonoured their girlfriends."

"How so?"

"Probably something I said…"

"Oh yes, Roy?"

"Yes, that's what it must have been. I asked them how much they charged for an evening." We both fell about laughing.

"I suppose it could have been that", I said, tears running down my cheeks, but with laughter this time.

Our laughter attracted other guests and because we were laughing so much it set them all grinning, wishing to share the joke. Ron stood looking on, staring at us, smiling and slowly shaking his head.

I lay in bed that night with my thoughts running through the events of the evening. I smiled at Roy's bluff of going for his imaginary gun at the club. I liked it! I vowed to myself that I would get a gun the next day. The reason I hadn't bought one before was that I didn't know when and where I might be posted. I might not really need one, but now I was convinced that I must get one. It wasn't just a popular habit in Kenya to hoist a gun, now I considered it to be a damn necessity.

CHAPTER 5

The next day I bought a gun. When I went into the shop who should I meet but Anne's mum once again (surprise, surprise!). She said, "I'm just buying supplies. How are you, Cy?".

"Bearing up", I said. I enquired after Anne but she lent nearer to me and put her finger on my lips, smiled and shook her head slowly.

"Sorry," I said, "It was natural that I should ask".

"I know, Cy. I realise that. She is okay now! It's you we should be concerned about and it is about time that you bought a gun. I'd noticed that you never carried one. I assume that is what you are here for?"

"Oh yes."

Picking up a holdall she said, "Please look after yourself. Don't stick your neck out or do anything silly. God bless you!".

I wondered and suspected if she had heard anything about last evening!! It was very likely knowing her. As she was leaving she said to Ahmed behind the counter, "Look after this one, he is a very good friend of mine". Then with a big wink she went out of the shop and into the sunshine.

I purchased a .22 Italian Beretta automatic with a supply of high-velocity bullets. This type had stood me in good stead before. It was light and therefore, easy to handle from a shoulder holster. It was accurate and with high-velocity bullets, could do a good job.

When I paid Ahmed said, "There will be 15% off the price". I expressed surprise and thanked him for his kindness. He said, "I always deduct 15% for Pen's special friends". So that was Anne's mum's name.

Penelope? Penny? No, just Pen! That really suited her. I had never thought to ask as she was always just 'Mum' to me. I wondered to myself where, when, or if she will pop up again. Things seem to get solved and sorted when she turns up!!

I settled into life at the annexe. There were two bathrooms with showers to be shared. There was no such thing as en-suites then. The family in room No. 1 seemed to live in the first bathroom. So much so that I never attempted to go in there. Even if I did go in the kids would come banging on the door so I never attempted to use it. If the second one was engaged I just hopped from one foot to the another until it became vacant. It was a primitive form of bladder control.

The family were very sociable and consisted of Mavis and William with their two children. Little Alice was about eight years old and who I imagined to be the original chatterbox! Blonde and blue-eyed, she was full of questions and full of answers. Godfrey, aged ten, was somewhat quieter and was conscious of the fact that he was a boy and felt vastly superior to his little sister. Mum and Dad were very ordinary, nice people.

Bert and Helen in room No. 2 kept themselves to themselves. They weren't anti-social but reserved. He was a little bit tubby with receding hair and Helen was dark with a figure like a beanpole. Both I guessed were in their thirties. They were rather nondescript people with not a lot of personality showing through.

Roy and I enjoyed the luxury of being driven to and from work by our resident chauffeur, Alec, in his little old banger. When we weren't out on the town, Roy and I had to buckle down to study with both of us being on a Swahili learning curve. He was on the same employment terms as I so it was logical to study together, either in his room or mine, with a refreshment to hand. We discovered that there were no swear words in Swahili so we had to invent some for ourselves.

The Mau Mau situation was getting worse. Many farmers had been murdered even though very rigid precautions had been put in place. Some of the Kikuyu who were the predominant tribe in and around Nairobi (and were the same tribe as the Mau Mau) were also being murdered if they were not cooperating with them. Many were forced to take the Mau Mau oath which was a vile ritual and if the recipient did not obey the command of the oath, they firmly believed they would actually die. As a consequence, many houseboys (who had been loyal for many years) were turning against their employers and destroying them!

We were all conscious of this changing situation and could feel the gradual increase in tension, especially so when Roy and I walked to and fro on our occasional nights out. We couldn't prise Alec out with his transport to come with us. I think he thought we were completely mad.

On Saturdays Roy and I would normally go to Nairobi for a day trip. However, on this particular day, Roy wasn't feeling well so we decided to stay and see if he improved before venturing out later. He had a tummy bug which can be debilitating. I was wondering how to occupy my morning when William called to see me.

He said, "It may be nothing, Cy, but the houseboy who normally comes to tidy up and do the necessary chores hasn't turned up to work. He hasn't missed a day in all the time that I have been here!! Do you think there is any significance in that?".

Facetiously, I said, "Perhaps he's got Roy's tummy bug! No! I don't think there is anything to worry about. He may turn up later". I thought, 'Everyone is getting so jittery — they must be getting Alec-itus!'.

I had a light lunch in my room and fed Roy with the odd brandy and milk during the afternoon, just to show that he wasn't forgotten. Then William called again. He said, "I know Little Alice is a chatterbox and romances things, but she says she saw an African's face looking in from the bush. She often looks through the windows at the birds and she swears that she was telling the truth". Why on earth does he think that he has to come and tell me? But taking the two happenings together it could be reasonably significant. I thought about it for a while and later on, I decided to ring the police for their opinion.

I went across the hall to the communal call box and picked up the phone. The line was dead!! Too much of a coincidence? Oh yes!! I think we may have a problem. What to do? It now had become quite reasonable to assume that we may be a target, and quite an easy one, viz. in the middle of the night when everyone is in a deep slumber. That was the Mau Mau's favourite time. Stealthily and quietly, they would probably be let in through the door by the houseboy to hack us all to death in our beds, including the kids! If that was their plan, we will have to stop it from succeeding.

Was I going over the top? Or was there a simple explanation for each happening? Was it Little Alice's imagination running wild? Was she perhaps seeking attention? Was the houseboy just off sick or injured and so was unable to come to work? Was there just a simple telephone fault? It was too late now to do a line inspection because of the approaching darkness. Thinking of the children being hacked to death decided me to suggest that we go ahead to defend ourselves, just in case.

I went to see Roy. He wasn't at all well so I didn't bother to tell him. He wouldn't be much good in his condition with the surprise strategy that was forming in my mind. I asked William, Bert and Alec to a discussion in my room.

Outlining my plan I suggested that instead of waiting inside for our potential murderers to surprise us, we will surprise them!! We will split into two groups. All of us now possessed handguns including Alec.

Alec said in a far from firm voice, "I'll come with you, Cy".

"Okay then. The idea is to turn the tables on them. We must get into position before it gets dark, which won't be too long now. Bert and William will go into the left dense bush and wait until the attackers pass close by them through the narrow track. Alec and I will wait inside the right-hand bush and do likewise. We shall keep a bullet in the gun barrel, otherwise loading the barrel on their arrival will alert them to their danger.

"As soon as they have cleared the path and are into the clearance area around the bungalow they will be sitting ducks. If they don't come tonight we will just have had an uncomfortable night, but if they do come they'll never dream that the 'white man' would wait completely silent, outside, in the dark and in a bush. That will shock them! They also won't know that we have been alerted by events and will expect to take us by surprise, asleep in bed.

"Tell the ladies to go to bed at the usual time so as not to arouse suspicion, but not a word to the children."

With everything sorted we went out before it got dark and got into our allotted positions, making ourselves as comfortable as possible whilst being completely covered in the bush with the track close by. I had emphasised the importance of complete silence and said that it will probably be a very long wait, but the end result will be worth it.

Although I must say that not all were terribly happy about the situation as I think the married men would have preferred to stay in and fight near their missus. But I pointed out that with it being a wooden building, another option for the Mau Mau was to set the place on fire. Eventually, we all agreed it was a good, but uncomfortable scheme.

Laboriously, hour by hour the time dragged by. Alec was very good. Very good indeed. Not a sound from him. He had not raised any objection to taking part and was keeping very still. I was beginning to change my mind about our Alec. He was becoming quite brave. It was the other two who were reluctant, most probably missing their warm beds.

It was well into the night now, probably about 2:30 to 3:00 am. I was beginning to feel a bit crampy down one side and was thinking that perhaps I had got it wrong and that it was all going to be such a waste of sleep time. Also, the moon was up. Why would they come in moonligh—

BANG!

A shot rang out from William or Bert. Then there was a second almost immediately from their direction. At the same time, Alec's gun went off but it was pointing at the annexe and he gave a stifled cry. Then I heard a rapid running on the track. The sound disappearing in no time at all. I assumed that it must be the raiding party running away. What the hell has been going on? What was everybody doing?

We all came out of hiding and had a hasty spot inquest as to what had happened. William said he saw an African with a panga (machete) and pulled the trigger as a reaction.

Bert said, "I heard the bloke yelp and then I fired at him as well!". I thought to myself, 'What an undisciplined lot. What happened to the plan?'.

Then William said, "There were a few of them and when you fired as well they must have thought they had been ambushed by the police askaris so they scarpered".

I said, "I did not fire!! You should have let them move down past us into the open as previously arranged. Then we could have seen 'em off! What the hell were you firing at, Alec?".

"I don't know! When their shots rang out it made me jump and I pulled the trigger. Really, it was a sort of reaction."

"Your gun was pointing at the annexe, Alec!!" I said, "Ah well, the threat has gone! Let's go to bed".

I looked in at Roy. As I opened the door the hall light shone on him. He was sleeping like a baby. Then I called Alec. "Look where your bullet went, Alec", and pointed to a splintered hole in the wooden wall about 18 inches above Roy's bed. "It's a good job the old sod wasn't sitting up eh, Alec?" I don't suppose Alec slept during the rest of the night (or what little there was left of it). Poor old Alec, why does nothing ever seem to work for him!!

The police arrived later in the morning and estimated that there was a party of about five Mau Mau. There was quite a lot of blood so one of them had been winged.

Well, it was Sunday morning and Roy seemed a lot better after a good night's sleep, if slightly hungover with the brandy and milk I had poured into him. He gave me a funny look when I showed him the bullet hole.

"What the bloody hell have you been up to, Cy?" The expression on his face made me laugh and I was glad to see him better. "What have I missed?"

"A bullet, you drunken bum!"

CHAPTER 6

During the next few days, everything happened in this land of Bado kidogo. Bado kidogo is a cliché that symbolises the attitude of the population. Many times, one asked a question and was answered by 'bado' which meant 'wait' or 'in a minute'. Bado kidogo meaning 'in a little while' or 'not just yet'. I was as amused by this symbolism as I was with 'are you married or do you live in Kenya?'. Yes!

Everything happened seemingly so suddenly. An Askari presence was now kept near the annexe. Dear old Alec decided that he'd had enough and was returning home to the UK and Roy received a letter transferring him to Eldoret in Kenya. Regarding myself, I received notification from the administration requesting that I leave the Queen's Hotel and take up abode in Thika Road House — no, not in Thika! It was the name of a very large hostel mostly inhabited by expatriates, just outside of Nairobi. The remainder of the annexe residents were also requested to move, as according to the rumour circulating, the police Askaris were going to use it as a post/billet.

It was a little sad to say goodbye to Alec. I suppose I had come to regard him similarly as I would a little brother who needed protection. But he seemed relieved that he had made the decision and that he was now going home to the UK. His firm organised his transport to the airport and his flight home so after a firm handshake in the hotel foyer and a few joking pleasantries, Alec departed.

A few days later I went to the railway station with Roy to see him off. I knew that he felt the same as I did, that a mutual bond was being severed. We had been so compatible and on the same wavelength. I knew

I was going to miss his friendship and companionship. So, with a "Keep in touch" and "Look after yourself" he went on his way to Eldoret. My little world seemed to be changing day by day, which I could cope with, but I would miss Smithy. Two days later a car came to pick me up and took me to my new home, Thika Road House.

Thika Road House was comprised of a vast amount of well-appointed timber chalets. They were very comfortable and one didn't have to share. There was a good restaurant on-site and the whole place resembled a present-day holiday park. Transport was no problem because everyone gave everyone else lifts into Nairobi. I was taken there and back every day with no obligation. The point was that the majority stationed there had started without 'wheels' and understood the position of newcomers on the block. It was a very friendly place and as well as the good restaurant it had a good clubhouse, a nice, well-appointed bar and a comfortable lounge.

After I had been there for a week and made quite a few friends I asked about the hostel security, especially now that the national security situation was deteriorating and extremely serious. I raised my concern that all the chalets were built on stilts or blocks (similar in height to the present-day caravans in caravan parks). Whilst having drinks at the bar, when I pointed out to other residents that Mau Mau terrorists only had to put a torch under them with devastating results, they sat up and took notice. Everyone seemed to not think about security. All were very complacent, probably thinking of safety in numbers. As for myself, suddenly coming to the roadhouse I saw it through fresh eyes and was not lulled into a false sense of security. Also, the very sudden recent change in vulnerability had not really sunk in to make them aware of the potential danger. I thought differently and was concerned that such a massive target in the dead of night, with many in one place and no security guards, was a dream target for Mau Mau. Yes, if I was a Mau Mau chief I would welcome it.

The residents in the eight chalets in my block were aghast from my observations and agreed that we should organise a patrol for the block.

We soon started guard patrols from midnight until 6 am every night of the week. Word soon got around and others wanted to join in, but I said no.

"Form your own units so that we have more individual units and more patrols. Keep the units small. If the system gets too big it could become cumbersome and inefficient. If you are only responsible for chalets in your immediate vicinity you will take a more personal interest in their protection. It will soon come to the notice of the Mau Mau and send them a message that there are many armed patrols at the camp. The Mau Mau are only interested in easy defenceless targets!!"

Then, suddenly, Jomo Kenyata was arrested. I had met Jomo Kenyata many years before in Manchester at the Britannia Restaurant which was owned or managed by Jomo's brother. I had a mutual lady friend who introduced Jomo to me. I did not know of his standing in Kenya amongst his Kikuyu tribe at that time and had no thought whatsoever of going to Kenya. The reason why I remembered him was twofold. Firstly, I was impressed by his presence and his stature and secondly, it was the first time I had tasted curry, which further impressed me!

The security of Nairobi was now at stake. The news reported that the East Lancashire fusiliers had been sent to Kenya from the UK. From the roadhouse in the distance I could see troops moving across the tarmac at Nairobi airport. On the same evening, I received a telephone call from the administration to come into Nairobi immediately. How the devil was I to get there without transport? I could hardly ask anyone to drive me into Nairobi. Even if I asked someone, they would be very reluctant to do so at night, especially in the present turbulent situation.

Ah well!! Here it goes. I walked through the gates in pitch-black darkness, onto the roadside verge and then stayed motionless. I was very aware of the possible attention from the wildlife but didn't expect anything large and dangerous to come close to the roadhouse with its associated noise and activity. No! I felt I had to be more aware of snakes in the darkness.

I had seen lights intermittently in the far distance, miles away and presumed that they might well be a vehicle traversing a hilly road. It seemed like an age before it became definite, but gradually it got nearer and I could distinctly hear the engine. I wondered who would be on the road at night given the present situation. Any vehicle travelling on the road would have a good reason for so doing and I also thought of my position standing there.

Suddenly, I thought about the approaching vehicle and hoped it wasn't full of Mau Mau who had decided to become motorised. Shudder!! These negative thoughts generally surfaced when I was alone and in the darkness. It was obvious the vehicle was in one hell of a hurry. As it approached at high speed I flagged it down. It took a while to stop with well-applied brakes. It was a camouflaged army staff car and as I opened the passenger door an army captain shouted from the driving seat, "Are you a bloody communist?".

"No," I said, "I am not".

"Get in then. Rather you than me standing on the road. I heard you bloody Kenyans are mad and now I know!!"

As we sped off to Nairobi I just couldn't tell him I was a mad Englishman like himself. I also did not ask him to explain the communist remark, yet I have always remembered it. Probably because it was such a very odd question to ask.

On arrival in Nairobi, I reported to my HQ. As I was standing there a truck appeared and the driver asked us how many we were. "Eight of us are here and registered as present", said someone with a pen in his hand. The driver then handed each of us a rifle and box of ammunition!

"You don't need to sign, it will all be allocated to each building. Get on the roof and cover each direction. There is talk that it will be 'the night of the long knives' tonight!!" And with that morale-boosting remark he sped off to his next customer.

It intrigued me briefly that it was so natural here in Kenya to automatically assume that everyone knew how to handle a rifle. Imagine in the UK; the signing of forms, the enquiries and the proof that you were capable and knew how to handle such a weapon before issue.

I looked at the rifle with nostalgic affection, smoothing my hand over the stock and the barrel. It was the .303 Ross rifle. The first time that I saw and used the Ross was when I was aged 17 in the Home Guard. But at that time we were known as the Local Defence Volunteers (LDV) prior to being named the Home Guard. We proudly wore an LDV armband to prove it. I mustn't digress!! That is another story.

We spent the remainder of the night on the roof as I suppose others were likewise doing on their bit of roof. Everything remained quiet until the Lancashire Fusiliers entered and took possession. I thought 'God Bless 'em'. Not just because they had relieved us from duty, but due to another nostalgic link. I came originally from their part of our beloved England.

I had become part of a group of friends at the roadhouse and spent some pleasant and interesting times with them. One of the Kenyan girls was a stenographer in one of the ministries and helped me enormously with my Swahili homework, which Abdul set me regularly.

I was over the moon when out of the blue I received my posting. "You will proceed by rail to Kampala, Uganda, where duties and your appointment will be detailed to you." Whoopee!! A journey into the 'interior' hundreds of miles away. What a dream posting!! I had been in Nairobi and district for six months which I thought was ample time to serve my 'apprenticeship'.

I rushed into Nairobi to say my goodbyes to the staff and also to Ron. I thanked him for all his help and kindness whilst under his roof and he laughed and said, "You do seem to stick your neck out don't you, Cy? Just be careful that you don't get it chopped off". I grinned at that and asked him to say goodbye to Pen for me. He said, "You can say goodbye yourself, she's with a ladies party in the lounge".

"I can't go in amidst that lot," I said, peering into the hotel lounge. "Hold on, I'll get her for you," he said.

Pen came in smiling. "What a situation we are in, Cy. It's quite funny at the Nairobi boundary. We were just talking and laughing about it. No African is allowed into the capital carrying a weapon, yet the Masai just walk straight through carrying their spears." I did laugh at that. I could picture a Masai, a very tall, dignified, proud warrior type dressed in just a blanket drape, carrying his spear. Nobody in his right mind would ever dream or risk attempting to take his spear from him!! They are quite fearless and helped the Kenyan police to track the Mau Mau at one period. Rumour has it that they not only tracked them but killed them and the police authority had to abandon the arrangement.

"You would have made a lovely mother-in-law, Pen."

"It just wasn't to be, Cy", she said. Then, after a big hug she wished me bon voyage and with that, we parted.

CHAPTER 7

When some of my roadhouse friends heard that I was going to Uganda by train on Saturday they said, "We can give you a send-off on Friday evening. You will be able to lie in on Saturday morning because you won't need to catch the train from Nairobi at 10:30. We will take you to Nakuru instead. The train doesn't depart from there until 3:30 pm". The gradients the locomotive had to negotiate were very time consuming and accounted for the lengthy time it took to reach Nakuru. Although it was 80 miles away, Nakuru was just a quick car hop by East African standards.

The 'gang' were very enthusiastic. "We will all go in our cars to Nakuru. It is a tarmac road most of the way, built by Italian prisoners of war in the 1940s." I could agree to do it because my compartment was reserved and paid for and would remain locked until I arrived at the train. Secretly I would have preferred to go from Nairobi to experience the torturous gradients and interesting views as the train descended the escarpment down to the Rift Valley. But the gang were adamant.

"No, you can't do with getting up early after celebrating the night before!! Oh, no! Besides, it is the done thing not to 'train it' to Nakuru." In the end, I had to bow to tradition. It was all part of my learning curve in East Africa.

Friday evening came and the place was crowded. No, I can't be that popular. No, I think it was just a good reason for a celebration. Any good old reason would do!

Through the haze of a very long evening I remember many friendly handshakes and slaps on the back. Bon voyage was both shouted and spoken softly. And I received the most acceptable, slightly inebriated kisses from the female stenographers! Well into the evening I thought it would be an excellent idea to go away once a week. That, of course, was while I was imbibing. The following morning would inevitably see a change of mind.

I don't know what time I hit the sack. Although I am one of the fortunate few who do not get severe hangovers, I felt relieved that I had not got to board the train at 10:30.

Abdul called to see me after breakfast. He was often at the hostel giving Swahili instruction. During his visit he gave me the name of a Swahili instructor in Kampala. It was his cousin, also named Abdul.

"You will like him, Cy. Make sure you do because between you and me he is one of the Swahili examiners." Then, with a funny little underhanded type of grin (that denoted we shared a secret that could be exploited), he shook my hand, left me in the care of Allah and was gone.

After lunch, we left the hostel in a convoy of cars and headed for Nakuru. Weaving down the escarpment we passed a rough-looking family of baboons.

Walter, a passenger in the car said, "Don't ever stop to look at them, Cy. They will jump on your car, muck and pee over it and besides scratching and damaging your paintwork they will twist your windscreen wipers so you hardly recognise them. An open car door would be catastrophic! They can be quite dangerous". Then, he pointed out a tiny, beautiful church, which was built by the Italian prisoners of war when they tarmacked the road between Nairobi and Nakuru.

After we dropped down to the Rift Valley it seemed a lot warmer. It was noticeably flat and vast. Endless, in fact. I saw railway tracks crossing the road and disappearing into the distance. The tracks appeared again and it was explained to me that it was the laborious way the train had to negotiate, by weaving its way, to traverse the terrain and descend the escarpment. A wonderful feat of British engineering to overcome what must have been almost impossible problems.

I had heard about its construction from Anne during one of our many tête-à-têtes as to how it was constructed in the late 1800s by British engineers. The huge monetary cost was borne by the British government during Queen Victoria's reign and there was also a terrible amount of lives lost. Over 2000! They were mostly labourers due in most part to man-eating lions in the Kenya section. It is no wonder that it earned itself the title of the 'Lunatic Line' in Britain during its construction. Anne also told me that Tsavo, a small station on the railway (and also the name of a game park there), means 'slaughter' in one of the tribe's vocabulary. Aptly named I think.

As previously mentioned, the great Rift Valley seemed so very flat and vast. It was a great savannah that stretched as far as the eye could see. It was approximately 20 million years ago that this large crevice in the earth's surface was created by unimaginable volcanic eruptions. We passed Mount Longonot on our left which stood out in marked contrast to the surrounding country. I thought that a magnificent view would be had from the top but of course, there was no time to spend viewing. It was an extinct volcano and would take some time to climb up to its crater edge. I was told that deep inside the crater wild game including buffalo resided. It would have been great to have taken the risk for a peep of them and the view, of course.

We slowed down near Naivasha then stopped inside the town. Likewise, the remainder of our company in their cars. It was another tradition to stop here to have a lager. I say inside the town, but actually, the 'town' was situated either side of the main dusty road. The only road. It reminded me of a scene in a Wild West movie as I walked through the rough, waist-high wooden swing doors looking for a litre bottle of lager. There was no gold inside, of course, except for the ice-cold lager in a crystal-clear glass. This was our liquid gold.

Substantially refreshed we continued on our journey, passing the shimmering lake Naivasha on our left. As we approached nearer to Nakuru, I saw the lake. Lake Nakuru. It looked pink with all the 'millions' of flamingo there. It was a most wonderful sight in the shimmering heat but there was no time for stopping, of course. I was catching a train!

We eventually arrived at Nakuru station. I did not expect the station to be so crowded and with such a lot of activity. Walter and Tim, the driver, took my suitcase from the car whilst I inspected the train. It was so very long, and the massive Garret locomotive had a 'cow catcher' and floodlight on the front, and a siren that sounded similar to the American trains.

As I made my way down the platform nearer to the third class section and the two luggage trucks at the rear, I was met with a constant happy noise of laughter, good-natured shouting and excited activity coming from the Africans that were gathered there. I had to negotiate a minefield of wicker baskets, clothes bundles and other paraphernalia that resided on the platform. The happiness surrounding them was infectious. Mabibi (African ladies) were parading up and down the platform bearing fruit, drinks and other goodies for sale for the journey ahead. Watoto (children) with the contrast of ebony faces and lovely white teeth, had beautiful big eyes, full of a mixture of wonderment and excitement.

I eventually negotiated my way back to the other half of the train and although there was lots of noise, it was nothing like as raucous as the third class passengers. We found the cabin with my name in the slot on the door and it was unlocked by one of the officials. It was time to board. I expressed my thanks to all gathered there for their help and friendship. Then the whistle went and the sound of the train's siren signalled my departure as we slowly moved out of Nakuru station.

I looked back, waving like so many on the train were doing. I saw such a lot of happy expressions. There were cheers, shouts of good luck, some shouting rude remarks (as a form of goodwill), and 'bon ami' expressed, understood and accepted from a herd of extrovert males. Eventually, I moved away from the window.

I mused over the superb bunch of friends I had. I felt that my life had been enriched by them and by all the other people in Kenya, just by knowing them. Even though they will undoubtedly pass like ships into the night.

So once again I was journeying into unknown territory. But there won't be any Mau Mau this time. I took stock of my surroundings. There was quite a narrow corridor down one side of the coach. My compartment was very comfortable with a well-upholstered bench seat, a drinking water tap, a mirror, a washbasin with soap and a towel, a sliding mesh insect window and a bell for service. The décor was very impressive. Luxurious, in fact, with fittings of walnut and maple veneers. The opposite wall looked as though concealed a convertible bed.

I would have to get used to the carriage with its excessive rolling, sometimes very excessive due to the narrow-gauge rails. I think it would have rocked when stationery, given a slight breeze!

For quite some time we had been climbing very slowly, up and up and up. I slid open the window and put my head out. We were on a curve and the edge of the track did not seem to be more than a yard from a sheer drop that looked bottomless. I thought, 'How the hell did the engineers carve this track out of the face of the mountain?'. We were rolling hideously from side to side and I could see the locomotive in the distance, slowly powering its way forward at walking pace, as up and up we went. Turning my head, I could see the other end with the luggage vans in the distance and — I could hardly believe it — there were Africans clinging to the outside of the luggage vans hitching a lift!

It was almost 6 pm and darkness suddenly arrived. There was no twilight nonsense so near to the equator. I had booked an early dinner and was beginning to feel in need of refuelling when I heard this delightful, simple, tinkling little tune. A few notes were repeating themselves and were getting nearer. As it got louder, I peered out into the corridor and espied an African waiter in a spotless kanzu, a green fez and cummerbund, and a dulcimer hanging from his neck. His hands, which were in white cotton gloves, were tapping the keys with tiny drumsticks announcing first dinner sitting throughout the coaches.

The dining car was well appointed with white tablecloths and silver service. I was shown to a table where I was to sit opposite a lady. We introduced ourselves. She gave her name as Emily Richards and I estimated her to be in her mid-thirties. She was quite severely dressed with a nice complexion and no makeup. She was very pleasant and complete with a formal smile. The conversation matched her smile and no encouragement was offered by her to make it otherwise.

The waiters were obviously well-trained, efficient and polite. I had consommé followed by delicately cooked tilapia lake fish with trimmings. It was absolutely delicious and had a distinct flavour so different from salt water fish, especially when so well presented. This was followed by an East African curry with all the special side dishes, as was the norm in East Africa. Because I am not normally a sweet course man, a nice glass of wine completed the excellent experience of my first East African train meal.

When I returned to my compartment I found it transformed. The bed was now out of the opposite wall and was covered in white, crisp cotton sheets that were neatly tucked in and turned to one side near the pillow as an invitation to sleep. A neatly folded blanket complemented the make up. Yes, a blanket!! It was to be needed later.

The train had stopped previously, but now it had reached its highest point at Timboroa at around 9,000 feet. I got out on to the platform to stretch my legs. It was freezing cold and the beautiful, big moon contrasted with the sky. Myriads of stars were against the pitch-black backdrop. The landscape, with its peaks and rugged appearance, looked moon-like and eerie. I did a few stretches, but not for long. I soon returned to the warmth of the train.

Instead of suffering my own company in the cabin, I went to investigate the possibility of other fellow passengers being present in the dining/lounge coach. A few characters were hanging around in the coach, including Emily. She must have felt conspicuous sitting there by herself because I was given a very pleasant smile which I interpreted as 'come and join me please'. So, I did!

Emily said, "I have just come in here. I thought it better than sitting alone in my compartment and was wondering whether I should stay. When you came in I hoped I would have your company". She had loosened up considerably after a drink. The severity disappeared and she became positively friendly. Not that friendly. She told me she had been on holiday in Mombasa and was driven there by friends from Kampala. After one week in Mombasa, they had driven back to Nairobi where she boarded the train for her return to Kampala. It was the first time she had been on a train in East Africa. She told me that it was a good idea health-wise to take a break on the coast after being upcountry for any length of time. She also told me that she was dedicated to nursing. She was a nursing sister who believed and practised a strict hospital routine and expected her staff to do likewise.

She loosened up even more after another drink and told me that she had looked out of the window earlier and was horrified at the sudden drop and how high we were. The terrible lurching and rolling petrified her.

"I've always been scared of heights", she said. "I don't like this rolling do you, Cy?"

"I can put up with it as long as I don't roll out of my bed, Emily", I said, recognising the use of Christian names for the first time.

I felt like putting my arms around her and telling her not to worry but I knew that would be far from welcome. As for offering to stop her from rolling out of bed in her cabin, it would probably have an even worse effect on her than one of her junior nurses dropping a bedpan on the ward! Although she had become nice and friendly, I gathered she had her principles and would abide by them. She would make a loyal friend —

platonically of course!!

Looking out through the lounge window I saw we had stopped at Eldoret. I thought of Roy and wondered how he was settling in. I believed he was living somewhere out of Eldoret on the Kakamega road. I also thought of my Mum and Dad and other friends at home that were probably relishing a nice cup of tea at this time in the evening. Being the norm, when offered a drink in the evening here it would be alcohol-based.

We, of course, went our separate ways to our cabins to sleep. I appreciated the addition of the blanket and soon fell asleep despite the rolling.

The early dawn and continuous rolling woke me. I gathered that we were through Tororo and approaching Jinja on the edge of Lake Victoria. Jinja is home to the source of the Nile, a location that I was determined to see. I missed my shower facility and had to make do with the washbasin. What with the water pressure, the small size of the washbasin and the physical cavorting to compensate, washing took quite a considerable time. Just before being summoned for breakfast, I noticed that the air had become much hotter and humid, more so than I had experienced in Kenya even though it was still quite early in the day.

I joined Emily who was looking out of the corridor window and received a nice friendly "Good morning". The train was tottering along with a soothing, slow clickety-clack with the bushy landscape slowly passing us by when we saw an African male standing stationary, having a pee and looking at the train. Before I could say something facetious or something to offset Emily's embarrassment, Emily quipped, "I suppose he thinks it pays to advertise". Totally an unexpected, funny utterance from Emily. But of course, she was a nursing sister and had seen it all before. She also had a sense of humour which she allowed out to play on the odd occasion. I was still chuckling to myself as we wended our way down the corridor for breakfast.

We eventually arrived at Kampala. Two gentlemen were there to meet Emily, whom she introduced as Dr Milne and Dr Broady. I turned around on hearing my name called. After acknowledgement I grasped the outstretched hand being offered to me by a large, rotund and tanned gentleman who was dressed in a blue sleeveless shirt, khaki shorts and plimsolls, complete with a huge welcoming smile. "Syd Lamkin. Welcome to Uganda, Cy."

Introductions with Emily and the doctors ensued. Then, as we stood around waiting for our luggage, both Emily and I remarked about what a pleasant train journey it had been and mentioned the haul up to Tambora.

Syd latched on immediately, "It will be quite some time whilst the railway staff extract your luggage from the caboose at the end of the train. Come and look at the locomotive".

I could tell by his demeanour that he was addicted to railways. He was very enthusiastic about the Garratt locomotive, waving his arms in the air, ending in a great flourish as we arrived at the hissing giant.

"You see what makes it more powerful than your ordinary engine, don't you, Cy? It has two sets of driving wheels instead of one."

I could see the four driving wheels situated at the front, not under the boiler which is the usual place. The other set of four driving wheels were at the rear beyond the boiler which made the locomotive very much longer than a normal one. It is no wonder that it managed to haul such a massive amount of coaches up the gradients to 9,000 feet. I should imagine that it would be equivalent to two ordinary engines. Syd beamed at the monster engine, completely captured by it and explained more of its attributes. I had difficulty coaxing him away as I espied my luggage being wheeled along the platform.

After almost dragging Syd away we returned to Emily and the doctors. Now that we were reunited with our luggage, Emily said, "I will be staying in Kampala, Cy, so will no doubt see you around somewhere. Nice to have met you".

I thanked her for the pleasure of her company and being bold as is my nature (or assuredly was then), I bent and kissed her on the cheek. She positively smiled in appreciation, her face turning red as we parted. Mmm!! I wondered if I could have managed to stop her rolling out of bed on the train? Don't even think about it, Cy!!

CHAPTER 8

Ever since arriving at Kampala Railway Station, I had felt the heat. My first impression had been the heat and the very oppressive humidity! It would certainly take a lot of getting used to. My shirt was literally sticking to my back and I could hardly wait to get to the hotel for a shower and change of clothing — especially after the long train journey. I envisaged a priority shopping spree for short-sleeved shirts and a quick change into my shorts.

The administration had booked me into the Imperial Hotel which was quite a reasonably sized and well-appointed establishment. On the first evening, I left my shoes out to be cleaned and promptly lost them! Yet, it was a pleasant five-day stay.

I had some urgent shopping to do so I went into town and purchased replacement shoes from a 'shoe shop' on Kampala Road. Kampala Road was the main thoroughfare through the town centre from east to west.

It was not a shoe shop as we know it in the UK, oh no! Not in Kampala. This shoe shop was not full of white boxes displayed on shelves. Instead, it had the odd table with a sewing machine and assorted gadgets arranged on the top. Cobblers were sitting crossed-legged at ground level, cutting and shaping leather, stitching and nailing.

I was invited to sit down on a chair in the open-fronted shop whilst the Asian proprietor drew around my feet. After taking vital measurements, he said with a friendly smile, "I will have them ready for you tomorrow". Wonderful! I also purchased pairs of khaki shorts and other miscellaneous items. Anything that needed altering was done on the spot.

Khaki shorts paired with a khaki shirt was the normal working dress in Uganda. Wearing my Nairobi whites would be very conspicuous and the wrong type of dress. In Nairobi, Mombasa or the coastal regions it was customary to wear whites, so depending on what was worn could distinguish newcomers and visitors from the local upcountry characters.

Whilst on Kampala Road I purchased other items. Khaki shirts (with epaulettes and two flap pockets with buttons), cotton leisure shirts and lightweight slacks. Walking around the high street, rolls of multicoloured fabrics caught the eye, displayed from open-fronted premises which were evidently a prominent feature in Kampala. There were grocery shops, coffee shops with Ugandan-grown coffee, cafés and restaurants. Nearer the western end of the town (in the Masaka and Hoima direction) was The Athenian. Here, I found delicious, very small and very hot homemade meat pies that had delectably delicate pastry. They also offered samosas that were ideal for elevensies. Close by was the cinema where film screenings commenced at 9:45 pm!! It is somewhat cooler then.

Barclays Bank was also in evidence, which I found very convenient. 'Mr Barclay' always seemed to pop up in places in East Africa, which I thought was very enterprising. Coca Cola was another. Even in remote habitats in the bush, I would come across a Coca Cola sign with a few bottles for sale.

On the other side of the road from Barclays was The City Bar which was owned by a Dutchman. I found out later that it was a popular meeting place with an exceptionally good menu. Yes, Kampala in the 50s had something. It was a lovely, active town with people to match.

I was allocated a flat on the outskirts of Kampala. It was in a large block of two-storey flats situated high up on Kokolo Hill. It had a view over the surrounding countryside and part of the Kampala's suburbs. There was luscious, dark green, rich-looking vegetation everywhere.

I must mention here that Kampala was built on seven hills, sharing this distinction with Rome, which is also built on seven hills. The first of historical importance is Kasubi Hill, which is where the Kasubi Tombs of the previous Kabakas are housed.

The second is Mengo Hill where Kabaka's Palace is situated.

The third is Kibuli Hill, is home to the Kibuli Mosque. Islam was brought to Uganda before the Christian missionaries came.

Namirembe Hill is the fourth and features the Namirembe Protestant Cathedral. The Protestants were the first of the Christian missions to arrive.

The fifth is Rubaga Hill, where the Rubaga Catholic Cathedral is and was the headquarters of the White Fathers.

The sixth, Nsambya, was the Headquarters of the Mill Hill Mission.

The seventh is the little hill of Kampala. The hill of the Impala is where the ruins of Lugard's Fort were. This hill is where Kampala got its name. There are other hills, namely Nakasero, Makerere, Mulago, Tank Hill (where the water tank is, or was), and Kololo Hill, the highest hill.

Another distinctive feature (not only to Kampala but applying to all permanent buildings in Uganda), is that all the buildings have to be fitted with a lightning conductor by law. If you were scared of thunderstorms, it was decision time!

The flat itself was large and modern. It had lovely bay windows fitted with an insect-proof separate fitting to repel 'boarders' in case the window was left open. The rooms were large. Spacious, in fact. The first thing I noticed was that there was no fireplace to provide a focal point. We British them take for granted in our homes. Fires were not needed for heat, of course, the atmosphere did not need any help to stoke up.

I purchased a car from Brian, one of my colleagues who wished to sell his car before he left Uganda in a month. I bought it so that I could have immediate wheels and to be able to get around shopping. I could also host meals out, to portray my thanks for their hospitality until I had got my flat in order. Brian and his wife Kitty were in the same block of flats as I, so the three of us shared the car for the duration of their stay in Kampala. Initially, I had some meals and drinks there and became wary of their little daughter, Alex. A lovely looking little girl, as was her mother.

Alex was extremely mischievous and did everything that little girls of three should not do. I never felt comfortable if she was behind me, especially when I was sitting down. On the first encounter with this darling little girl, I had a pin stuck in the back of my neck, which felt like a dagger at the time. Great glee was exclaimed from the little angel when that happened. Another time, a quick sharp tug on my back hair which almost dislocated my neck was another uproariously funny game. Another 'funny' occasion was when Kitty, Brian and I left the room to look at something in the kitchen. When we returned, Brian and Kitty had cigarette ends and ash in their drinks and I had a very big, dead, sausage fly and a grasshopper in mine. A dear little child. I felt like putting her in the fridge.

I soon acquired a houseboy. His name was Manweri and he turned out to be very house-proud, conscientious and a good cook. We managed our verbal communication initially with pigeon English and pigeon Swahili. But it didn't help a lot because I was learning Kiswahili (the pure Swahili) in order to pass my exams, and he was speaking upcountry Swahili which everyone used in Uganda. It never seems easy does it? And God it was always so hot and sweaty. I was having a lovely time. Even in bed at night it was sticky.

There were so many flying insects. There were flying grasshoppers about two inches in body length, flying beetles, plus all the flies, of course. One Sunday, I mistakenly left the door open and sitting in the lounge I heard a loud droning noise. I wondered what fate awaited me. It was 'only' a big hornet, built like a Lancaster bomber with its undercarriage down. I played hide and seek with it for a while until I realised it wasn't hunting me. There were also sausage flies flying in about the same size as the hornet (the sausage fly is aptly named), but they weren't armed like the hornets. I didn't know that then so I had quite an athletic time. I seemed to be learning something every day. Don't leave the door open, Cy!!

There were ants everywhere of different sizes. A few crumbs or grains of sugar left on the floor and you would soon see an army of ants in long lines taking possession. At night there were cockroaches. They were 1 inch across, some even bigger, looking for anything edible. No matter how clean the place, they came from God knows where.

The night also brought out the loud African chorus. Frogs, crickets and many other different species of God's African insects, all chanting their songs to make up a great cacophony. The noise did take some getting used to. Of course, there were also snakes, they live here.

So, to recap. No doors to be left open, everywhere to be kept clean, worktops included. Don't leave any milk or any other perishables out for even a very short time or they would very soon go off.

I soon got used to the tiny flies in my drink and crawling on my face. I stopped swatting them otherwise I would have looked like a bruised boxer. And as for my shirt sticking to my back, so what the hell, just let it! After showering, the humidity was so high that no matter how much towel was applied, no evaporation seemed to take place and my shirt had to be pulled back on, sticking to the skin during the process. Just some of the little differences between Kenya and Uganda.

To complete the picture, on Sunday mornings massive drums of the cathedral situated on Namirembe Hill, would be heard echoing and rolling around the hills and valleys calling worshippers to morning service.

Enjoy, Cy!! And yes I was!! This to me was real Africa.

CHAPTER 9

I had only been in my flat for a couple of days when I bumped into Emily coming out of the flat next door. Surprise surprise!! Unbelievable! Emily was my next-door neighbour!! A small world indeed. She invited me for afternoon tea that same afternoon, which I thought was very hospitable of her.

I arrived promptly at the allotted time and could see that Emily had a well organised flat, just like I imagined a nursing sister would have. Everything was so neat and tidy. We seemed to have so much to talk about whilst munching our way through salmon and cucumber sandwiches which were cut into triangles and so nicely presented. During our conversations, she told me she was going into hospital as a patient in a few days and may have to stay in there for a little while. I enjoyed the afternoon with Emily and although invited to stay longer I regretfully had to leave before dinner to shower, change and meet my new Swahili teacher, the new Abdul.

Abdul was an Arab and similar to his cousin in Nairobi. He was more vocal and gesticulating but just as friendly. At the end of the lesson, he said that I would be able to pass my elementary grade by the following week.

To test Manweri's skills I invited Brian and Kitty for dinner. Alex would be in bed — 'Praise be to Allah!!' — and would be watched over by her Ayah (African nursemaid). Manweri, dressed in his white kanzu and broad green cummerbund really showed off his skills by cooking a lovely dinner and expertly waiting on the table. I was very pleased with the effort he had made.

It was quite late when Brian and Kitty left and before they went, they congratulated me on my good choice of houseboy. When I went into the kitchen, Manweri still hadn't finished clearing up, so I said, "It is late and you have worked so hard, Manweri. Go home and I will finish off here". He hadn't far to go. The houseboy's quarters were separately situated behind the property.

The next morning, Manweri was not happy. He was quite sullen in fact and no matter how hard I tried I couldn't solve the problem. I called Brian in the next evening to help language-wise and all was revealed. Manweri had taken exception to me taking over his duties and asked if he was not cleaning the dishes properly. Brian, in his more advanced Swahili, explained the situation to him. To me, he said, "Houseboys take great pride preparing dinner, especially when you invite guests. They just love to dress up in their kanzu and show off their skills, so it is belittling to them when you step in before he has made everything spotless again". If I had been in Manweri's place I would have welcomed any help to clear up. So, the learning curve once again. Thou shalt not interfere!!

Later, I had a look inside the main Kampala Communications Building to see what my work would entail. I inspected the equipment and the geographical sites of exchange satellites. These were small exchanges serving communities outside Kampala and were unmanned. There were four of them all out in the 'Bundu' in different directions. A problem at any of them would operate a 'prompt' emergency alarm in the main Kampala auto exchange. After normal working hours when the exchange was not staffed, all the alarm circuits (including the main Kampala auto exchange) would be switched to the telephone operator staff. If any of the alarms were activated they would call out the emergency engineer by telephone.

The following Sunday lunchtime I decided to visit Emily in hospital at Nakasero. I couldn't believe it when I went into the ward. Emily was sitting up in bed and around the bed were four ladies and three men. Two I recognised as Dr Bob Milne and Dr Bill Broady, whom I had met at the station.

Emily looked up and beamed when she saw me. "Ah come in, Cy. What would you like to drink?" Bill went to the table and said, "Gin? Beer?". Everyone had a glass in their hand and was laughing and chatting away. I soon had one in mine. Such a nice Sunday lunchtime party in progress. Then I noticed the dog laying happily and comfortably next to the bed, probably having a break in the middle of his walkies. So, this was it, hospital Uganda-style. Something matron would not have approved of back home!!

Bob Milne said to me, "The young African nurses are so very attractive in their new nurse's uniforms. You must get yourself in here as a patient, Cy".

Emily very quickly quipped, "Oh no, I lost two nurses last month. Pregnancy is an occupational hazard to them!"

I said, "Thank you, Emily". The inference was not lost on me. Emily and her quips!

During my visit, which was a very pleasant one, I noticed the 'nursing sister' surfacing in Emily when Bob put the gin bottle on the floor next to the cabinet. She said, "Put it on the cabinet, Bob".

Jokingly Bob said, "Oh it's okay there, Emily. It can't fall very far on the floor".

Emily with piercing, unwavering blue eyes said, "There is a place for everything and everything in its place". This was one of Emily's nursing sister bible phrases. With a sheepish grin in my direction, Dr Bob promptly restored the gin to its rightful place. Yes, Emily has obviously got the doctors sorted.

At the beginning of the week, I passed my elementary Swahili examination quite easily but I was warned that the later examinations would be more comprehensive and much stricter. I felt that I was getting really well advanced and could speak the language without having to translate it in my head first.

The same day that I passed my Swahili examination I received an invitation to His Excellency, the Governor of Uganda's garden party in Entebbe, the seat of government. Brian and Kitty likewise! No invite for darling little Alex… What a shame!

CHAPTER 10

Acceptance to His Excellency, the Governor of Uganda's garden party was a must. The only time you could refuse the invitation was if you were deceased.

I went to see Brian and Kitty to discuss our invitation but they were already in a heated discussion regarding a dress. I could see that Kitty was quite excited. She was a naturally excitable person to begin with and of course she wanted to have a new dress and hat. Brian disagreed. The expense of such an exercise would be a serious invasion into his hard-earned savings. He was clever but obstinate, very forgetful and was often sent to the dog house by fiery Kitty. Of course, little Alex took great delight at every opportunity to benefit from such an occasion.

When I first witnessed a confrontation, I excused myself to save embarrassment. But no, "Stay, Cy", they said. They were quite happy to air their problems in front of me. It was just a way of life to them and surprisingly I soon got used to it. In fact I was amused by it, similar to visiting the cinema.

It was obvious that Kitty would have her dress and hat. Any sane man (other than Brian) would have accepted the inevitable as soon as the invitation was received. It was a 'woman thing' of paramount importance. To refuse such a request could result in a long sentence of penal servitude in the dog house and probably the 'mean and nasty' stigma would stick and resurface on numerous occasions thereafter.

Kitty was cock-a-hoop the next time I saw her. "I've got my dress", she exclaimed triumphantly whilst waving the carrier bag. "And a gorgeous hat as well. Come and see, Cy!!"

The dress and hat made Kitty deliriously happy and after parading in front of us so that we could register our approval, she decided that she would have to take it into town for a slight alteration.

On Saturday morning, the morning of the garden party, I, suitably attired, arrived at their flat in plenty of time and walked into the beginning of a massive confrontation. The flat smelt awful. It transpired that Kitty went to pick up her altered dress leaving Brian in charge of Alex. He was sat in the chair repairing someone's toaster at the time. We were often called upon to repair domestic appliances in the community. It was the done thing to help one another. Brian evidently had had a disturbed night and succumbed to a little bout of shut-eye.

Kitty arrived home and the first thing she said was, "What is that awful smell? What has been going on?". Brian, so befuddled after being suddenly and rudely awakened just did not know. "Where's Alex?" Brian did not know!!

Kitty flounced into the bedroom and found Alex there. She had used her potty, tipped it on to the carpet and smeared it on the walls with her fingers, drawing pictures. It was also on the bed and bedroom furniture. "I can't trust you to do anything," Kitty raged at Brian, "Even simple little things. You can't even look after your own daughter just for a few minutes".

Kitty switched on her iron and arranged her dress for pressing, still raging at Brian. Brian looked quite contrite and resigned to Kitty's broadsides. Then Kitty, leaving her pressing and propelling me into the bedroom, said, "Look at this to be cleaned up, Cy!! Just look at it". I agreed with her it looked and smelt a mess.

I excused myself to return to my flat for half an hour to give them some space, and to give me a few lungfuls of fresh air. When I returned it still smelt awful but was now tinged with a heavy antiseptic presence. As I stood inside the doorway I could see that Kitty was looking crestfallen and near to tears. "Whatever is wrong, Kitty?", I said.

With a quivering lip, she replied, "I've cleaned everywhere including Alex, but it does not smell right. And look at this!". She held her dress up for me to see, showing an iron scorch mark in the front. Then suddenly, with venom in her eyes, she swung the dress around, waved it at Brian and shouted, "I can't wear this, it's all your fault!".

Brian, already deep in the dog house and in self-destruct mode dug himself in deeper by saying, "You shouldn't have left the iron on it". Kitty looked as though she was about to explode as she flounced out of the room clutching her dress.

Alex, looking all polished and clean after her thorough decontamination, was enjoying the whole scene, albeit knowing that she was centre stage. Thanks be to God that Alex would be staying at home with her Ayer.

There was nothing we could do about the dress. Although it was singed, the damage only measured about three inches square so after a calming, healing interlude, a solution to the problem was found. As a damage limitation exercise, Kitty must hold her small 'dressy' handbag just below her naval at all times to hide the patch.

I drove to Entebbe thinking of self-preservation because they were still a bit niggly with each other. After a few miles Kitty, mostly on the offensive suddenly burst forth like a volcanic eruption when Brian, already on the edge of disaster said, "You've ruined the dress, what a waste of money it has been". I don't know how we managed to get to Entebbe without a serious crime being committed but we did.

On entering the grounds at Government House, we joined the others in an orderly, shuffling line towards the garden entrance, awaiting our turn to be presented to His Excellency and his wife. Eventually, the cards were taken from us and our names proclaimed in a loud voice. After shaking hands and exchanging pleasantries we passed through to join the mass of multicoloured hats and dresses drifting around in the boiling hot sun. Amongst this mass of colour, white kanzu'd waiters weaved dexterously, skilfully balancing trays with liquid refreshment on them.

Brian was shuffling along looking bored, probably brooding as to the cost of this day out. Whilst Kitty, all bright and excited was in her idea of heaven and clearly lapping up every minute of the atmosphere. She kept her handbag clutched tightly to her naval and cleverly gave little odd waves to friends.

The Governor's Aide-De-Camp circulated amongst the guests and introduced himself to us. I didn't know at the time I shook his hand that I would see a lot of him and his boss in the future.

Eventually, we gravitated to a large canvas-sided enclosure. Various groups of people were standing engaged in polite conversation, sampling food taken from a great variety of fayre situated around the canvas walls on a 'continuous' table.

Suddenly a thin little black arm reached up from under the flap. After feeling around like a periscope under remote control, the arm silently removed a few buns from a plate and disappeared from whence it had come.

Being British and therefore not recognising out of depth, socially embarrassing situations, each and every one of us looked away and pretended it had never happened. Not Brian, however, coming from Liverpool. He loudly and indignantly proclaimed (in his best Liverpudlian accent), "Did you see that? A hand came up and pinched some buns!!".

Kitty, trying to live as much as she could above her station and eating from Brian's plate with one hand (because her other hand was still clasping her handbag tightly to her naval), admonished Brian with an attempted posh Liverpudlian, Westminster accent, "He has not pinched them, Brian he has taken them".

I hoped the little African boy enjoyed his buns and didn't get caught. If I could, I would have thanked him for the entertainment he had unwittingly provided.

Back in Kampala, upon entering Brian's flat it still smelt vile. I was so pleased I would be sleeping in my flat. It was a whole week before

Brian and Kitty discovered the source of the smell. Their little angel had pressed some of the contents of her potty into the brass narrow cups on top of the bedposts. Although it was a great relief to have found it, it was an extremely difficult task and very time consuming to remove it. Dear, dear Alex, 'sugar and spice and all things nice'? Don't believe a word of it!!

CHAPTER 11

I was beginning to earn my coin now. My Swahili was quite good verbally and I could converse quite well with African personnel. There were many Asians on the staff but the majority spoke English so there was no problem there. Because of this (and the fact that I'd had time to familiarise myself with the geographical area, the staff and the equipment), I was appointed as the Maintenance Control Officer.

The standard of maintenance was very low both externally and internally, especially in the Auto Room. I had lots to get my teeth into. This appointment, of course, coincided with the start of the rainy season, which was rather unfortunate. From March to May there were long rains and around November came the short rains. The temperature did not vary much but it 'stoked up' for Christmas.

With the rains came thunderstorms, the like of which I had never seen before. They were vicious and inflicted severe damage, especially to our communications. Maintenance, of course, suffered. The storms normally lasted about two hours more or less every day. The rain came down like walking sticks and it took the storm drains (which were built into the side walls of high kerbs) all their time to cope with it. Then the sun would come out and moisture could be seen rising from the ground as vapour. A few minutes later would see the ground dry again as the boiling heat from the sun took over. It was also the period when due to lightning strikes household electrical appliances were thrust upon me for repair.

Being acclimatised I was now able to sleep in the sticky, clammy humidity so it was inevitable that I had to be rudely awakened, the story of my life. The calamitous heavy crash of thunder shook me into reality. I opened my eyes to see lightning crackling around the metal mosquito netting on my bedroom window. Lying flat in bed, being the safest place, I stayed there. Just as I was turning my head there was a series of flashes on my pillow. 'My God, the bed had caught it', being my first natural understanding of the situation. It took me a few moments to realise that a firefly was happily showing its natural functional phenomena about two inches from my eye.

Amongst the almighty 'heaven-sent' thunder noise the phone rang.

"This is the operator speaking, sir. Red prompt alarms are showing for Mbuya, Mengo, Kawempe and Bombo!"

"Thank you," I said, always polite. He was only carrying out an essential part of the procedure. Nevertheless, I did say a little more than 'dear, dear' to myself.

It sounded like World War II raging outside as I pulled on my shirt and shorts. I looked into my shoes, turned them upside down and banged them on the bed framework, a good habit. There were such a lot of 'things'. Some good, some not so good, and some which were quite horrid and unpleasant, crawling and squirming around.

I must digress a little and tell you about one such microscopic nasty that lives on the floors inside and out. Anywhere, in fact, to catch you if you dare to prance around barefoot.

It is the Jigger. It bores into your foot leaving you in complete ignorance of its presence. It then lays its eggs in an egg sac beneath the surface of the skin, similar in size to frog spawn. If that egg sac is broken or punctured the eggs will run under the skin to other parts of your foot. You are then in deep trouble. Hospital doctors don't wish to touch them in case the sac is pierced. Go to the experts on the subject, i.e. any African. Give him a blunt safety pin and he, with great skill (he's been doing it for a lifetime) will dig around and around the sac. There is no pain as the area is dead. Then, he will deftly pierce the parent grub and lift the whole unit out intact. Applying paraffin to the crater completes the operation. Manweri has had the pleasure of me calling for that service twice.

So back to my call out. Before getting in the car which was in the dry area, I looked up into the sky through the heavy rain and almost continuous lightning. The nearest description as to what I saw was likened to a horizontal long comb with the thick top frame vividly lit. From this thick bar of light were a massive number of long brilliant white teeth urgently seeking the earth. It didn't hang there for very long but I thought of all that frightful natural energy. That was centre stage. There were many other 'normal' fireworks acting as part of the chorus.

Just as I was about to open the car door and in a fraction of a second of brilliant light I saw a snake on the ground just behind the front wheel. With my size tens I would have surely shocked him into a real grumpy mood. I threw a few bits of earth at him until he slowly slithered away. He wasn't attacking me so why kill him? He lives here and probably for a lot longer than I had.

So off to Mbuya, the first one I had to deal with. The rain was so heavy I could only crawl along because visibility was obscured by the rain and the wipers couldn't quite cope. Another factor was the lightning. After each local flash, there were quite a few seconds of blindness until my eyes readjusted to the pitch-black night.

At Mbuya there seemed to be millions of frogs and other noisy friends in a pond area all trying to compete with Dante's inferno going on around me. The lightning had tripped the generator in Mbuya exchange and the exchange was running on massive storage batteries. Each cell was comprised of a thick glass jar measuring approximately 18 inches by 18 inches and 2 feet deep. They contained sulphuric acid electrolyte in them and were all connected to each other to give the correct exchange voltage. The generator had to be restarted and gradually eased to the correct voltage.

When this was achieved, the large circuit breaker situated on a black, polished power board and complete with a black ebony insulated lever was slammed home. If it was not at the correct voltage it would fly out again. After the circuit breaker was locked in the generator would charge the batteries and keep them topped up. It was called the float system and a similar principle is used in cars.

Having dealt with Mbuya I had to drive out to the others. Bombo would be the furthest to tackle with whatever problems awaited me there. It wasn't a job I would choose. To go out in the middle of the night during a violent thunderstorm, pitch-black everywhere (except for sudden, blinding light) and having to use a torch to ensure nothing nasty was trodden on in my soaking, squelchy shoes whilst negotiating a narrow, muddy path amongst tall grass!

The remainder of the satellites were similarly affected and sorted out. Hours later I arrived back at the flat, peeled off my soaked bush shirt and shorts, towelled and jumped into bed. Oh luvly, luvly bed!! The storm was slightly abating. I'll sleep like a baby now, and felt very snuggly like one. Such utter bliss!! Then the phone rang!

"This is the operator speaking, sir. There are red prompt alarms for Mengo, Mbuya, Kawempe and Bombo." OH, NO NO NO!! Not again.

Eyeing my wet clothes hanging on a rack, I thought, 'I've got to get out of this haven and do it all again'. Then cynically, 'This is real Africa, Cy!! Remember?'.

CHAPTER 12

We were having a few problems in Masaka district. The district is spread over a wide area covering territory as far as the Belgian Congo, the Rwenzori Mountains and south to Tanganyika. The town of Masaka was only 80 miles southwest of Kampala, so I decided to spend a week there to see the staff, their organisation and what equipment they had.

Although my work and knowledge were centred on the technical side of communications, I did have to cover a broad spectrum of knowledge including a commitment to the external side, i.e. pole routes, wire, trucks, ladders etc. Masaka district was such a district. It had little in the way of technical equipment but very long lines of communication which were vulnerable to all manner of damage.

I booked into a small hotel in Masaka — it was the only one in the town — and had a good night's rest. All the staff were standing and waiting when I arrived in the building the next morning, probably wondering what the Bwana Mkuba (Chief Boss) would be like. I greeted them all with a smile and "Mjambo" (Hello) and received a chorus of replies in return. The officer who was normally in charge was off duty, sick. An African now in charge was holding the fort. He was quite respectably dressed, which I appreciated, and he spoke good English.

The rest of the staff were obviously external linesmen and spoke only broad Swahili, which I could easily cope with. Their dress was almost 'uniform', comprising of ragged shorts, different arrays of shirts, some khaki, and nearly all of which looked as though they had been in use for some considerable time. All, of course, were barefooted. They were basic characters, active and uncomplicated, which I liked. I said something funny to them in Swahili to break the mild degree of perceptible apprehension on meeting the chief Bwana. The reaction was quite dramatic. They slapped their thighs and laughed uproariously, obviously not used to a funny Bwana. So, friendship established, I turned my attention to look at the way the organisation was run.

As the morning progressed it became very hot, and I was glad to be dressed in a bush shirt, shorts and plimsolls. I was studying routine worksheets and other papers such as expenditure, with Jonathan, the African temporarily in charge. He told me that he had a missionary school education and that he had been working in Masaka for five years. He had good knowledge of the work, which impressed me.

At about 11 am, I had just had coffee and a pastry from the hotel when Jonathan told me that there was a fault on the main route to Bukoba in Tanganyika. He knew how to use the detector/oscilloscope and estimated that the fault was eight miles away. I noted it, then, on impulse said, "Hold on, I will go with the linesmen and truck and take a look at the standard of pole route maintenance on the way". It would fill in the time nicely until lunch. I thought Jonathan looked surprised and a bit taken aback by my decision. But, not being a total armchair technician I went outside and joined eight linesmen who were getting on the truck. It was an old Albion truck that was well loaded with poles, masses of wire coils etc. and had a floodlight and winch on the front.

Getting into the most uncomfortable driving seat imaginable was accompanied by, "Eh", "Ah", and "U-U-U-U" from the linesmen. They were all very surprised that the boss man was coming on the truck and not in his car, and even more surprised that I was in the driving seat. The truck started up and sounded like a load of marbles in a galvanised bucket. As I turned the steering wheel it turned almost full circle, before the road wheels responded. The costing of a new truck crossed my mind. Thank God, it was only eight miles!!

We trundled out through the small township, turned, and headed out onto the Bukoba road which was a long, hard-baked, ridged, murram road. Again, thank God it's only eight miles. I could hardly keep it on the road, wrestling with the free play in the steering wheel. I managed to raise the speed to lessen the continuous jolting, as we rode the corrugations.

After approximately eight miles of this torture, I told the bodies in the rear of the truck to look out for the fault. I hadn't seen anything amiss on the pole route up until then. They fell about laughing, saying, "Bwana mjinga", (Bwana joking/Bwana very funny). I thought such mirth for such a simple request. Not so much mirth on my part when I discovered that the fault was at mile eighty, and not mile eight. No wonder Johnathan had looked surprised earlier.

I said a sincere little prayer for my bum. My shoulders were starting to ache due to gallant efforts with the steering wheel trying to keep 'Grandma' on the road. Lunch would be missed, and I was hardly dressed for a safari in plimsolls. Then, shouts of "Poli poli, rafiki yangu Bwana!", (Slowly, Bwana, my friends!) as we approached a few of their ragged dressed friends, walking along the road. As we slowed down, they jumped on the truck. This practice was often repeated as deeper into the interior we went, passing the lakes and Kyotera. I also had to slow down to let them get off and it was beginning to resemble a country bus.

It was now mostly elephant grass and a few mud huts. 'Miles and miles of nothing' passed through my mind. Then, I started to sing, primarily to ease the pain in my bum. It was better than weeping. So, 'One man went to mow, went to mow a meadow', was sung in a loud, anguished voice. Then I sang it in Swahili, just for fun, only I had to modify it to 'One man went to dig, and went to dig the earth', because they did not mow grass in the wilds of Africa.

At first, there was silence as the words were absorbed, then gradually they all joined in. Great fun! The truck was full of linesmen and their friends, some hanging on the sides, all in great voice. Although physically thoroughly uncomfortable, I was enjoying the experience. Miles of nothing and a truckload of happy African voices giving it all they had got, trundling along this hard and dusty road in the hot baking sun in the middle of Africa.

As we approached each tiny village everyone was out on the road. They must have heard us coming from afar. All were curious, and wide-eyed watoto (children) looked astounded as we passed. Most of them waved and shouted, others just stared. I always slowed down at each village in case someone wanted off and someone wanted on.

Nearing Mutakula there seemed to be a celebration going on. Many of the villagers were on the road wondering what was coming. I was deep in it now. I was a really isolated white man in a completely different culture. "Goja hapa Bwana!", (Stop here, Bwana!). There were the heavy sounds of drums and lots of noisy shrieks as we pulled up. Then amongst this obvious festive occasion the faces near the road altered to a puzzled, suspicious look, as their eyes fell on the driver. Everyone near the side of the road became quieter, serious-faced, and stared with a certain hostility at my face. There was a lot of shouting. It was mostly a mixture of Luganda and Swahili between my passengers and the large group of villagers, who were stood around the truck and on the roadside. Some of my staff shouted wildly in Luganda language. They laughed and pointed at me, after which the stern and suspicious faces slowly broke into smiles. Some held out their arms to touch me as a gesture of friendship.

Everyone was getting off the truck now and I was just about to lay down the law (we had a job to do), when I realised they were standing facing away from the road… They were all having a pee. Somehow, I extricated myself from the apology called a seat and joined them. It was called 'seeing Africa'. I was more than ready to do so. The celebration had now resumed its original intensity and as my staff and I resumed our places upon the truck I had pieces of melon thrust upon me by some of the happy, smiling ladies of the tribe. With a lot of waving and sounding of the horn, we started off again on the Bukoba road.

We saw the fault after we had passed into Tanganyika and before we had got to the Kagera River. Praise the Lord! The pole route was some way off the road and was standing in tall elephant grass. One pole had been damaged, probably due to elephants coming from the river. The linesmen expertly moved the replacement pole from the truck, plus the tools, wire coils etc., but were reluctant to sally forth through a few hundred yards of elephant grass. They kept staring at me saying "Nyoka" (snake), and "Chui" (Lleopard) may be in there. No matter how hard I tried I could not persuade them to walk through the grass. So, against my better judgement and the only way I could get communications established, was to lead the way in.

I looked down at my plimsolls and bare legs and apologised to my legs for what I was about to put them through. It was decision time, and what I was paid to do. I would lead the way in and the staff would follow with the equipment. Everyone was happy with that arrangement. They would be! I couldn't blast them with a 'coward', or 'scared' tirade, because I did not know the Swahili for those expressions.

With much foreboding (and wondering why it was that I seem to attract such unwelcome situations), I entered the grass, stamping my plimsoll-enclosed feet on the ground to alert any sleepy snakes into moving away. The staff followed behind making much noise to hopefully scare anything big and nasty that might be lying in there contemplating lunch. It seemed such a very long, long walk, stepping my way through waist-high grass when eventually I arrived at the pole. In utter relief, I turned and gestured to them with great (but false) bravado and proclaimed, "I don't know what all the fuss was about".

They worked very well together and it was obvious that they had done it before. The pole was replaced, wires erected and regulated. I went up the pole with them and after they had used the ratchet, I showed them a simple way to balance the wires which was met with great approval.

What would they have done when it came to decision time to enter the grass if I had not been there? The one who drew the shortest blade of grass? Were they testing to see how brave Bwana was? Or if I was mug enough to take the risk instead of them? I just don't know. They were so straightforward that I don't think they were capable of being devious.

It had been such a relief to get my bum off that seat. So, with circulation having been restored to that part of my anatomy, plus much wheeling of the arms to free my shoulders, we embarked on the return journey. The same procedure was repeated as the outward journey, getting on and off at villages. The party at Mutakula was more subdued and appeared to have moved into the bush, away from the road. Nevertheless, there were quite a few characters by the roadside who waved and shouted as we slowed down on our way through.

Ten miles further on we came to the aftermath of a thunderstorm we had seen in the distance. The road had the consistency of porridge and the weight of the vehicle actually helped to keep us on the road. Plus the recently developed expertise with the steering wheel helped. The big-headed attitude was not to last long.

Approaching a rise in the road I saw another vehicle on top of the ridge descending towards us. Actually, it was an apology for a bus with no windows. It was crowded with the usual acrobats hanging on to the sides together with a vast number of green banana bunches. The body of the bus had evidently been refitted to a chassis, but not aligned properly, so one had the most uncomfortable feeling that it was coming straight at you. They were known as crab vehicles. The wheels were on a straight course, but the actual body was not. It was quite common in Uganda.

Then, consternation! The bus slithered from one side of the road to the other and appeared to be coming broadside on. There was only one thing to do, so off-road we went to miss this deadly missile and into a wide rut of running water. I stopped with both nearside wheels bogged down to the axle, the other two still in the porridge. The wretched bus recovered and stopped further down the hill. I would have had nightmares driving that thing. Grandma was bad enough.

Everyone was soon milling around in the porridge. There was a lot of noise, laughter and greetings between the bus characters and our linesmen. Quite a get together really. No sense of time, of course. All enquiring about the health of family and neighbours, seemingly such a happy event!! I had come to realise as I was observing this very social occasion that patience in Africa (as far as I was concerned) had now become a necessity and no longer a virtue.

There must have been hundreds of large bunches of bananas being extracted from the porridge, and packed onto the bus, plus a few nondescript bundles (no doubt worldly possessions) being restored to their rightful owners. When all the ritual pleasantries had been exhausted they all turned to the task in hand.

Whenever there is something heavy to be lifted, pulled or pushed, the Africans are masters. A cheerleader miraculously surfaces, gives voice with a run-up of sounds, ending with an accentuated end voice. It is at this endpoint that power is applied, all taking part with gusto. Consequently, the amount of effort is concentrated at the same time and so it was in this case. With the manpower from the bus plus our own, accompanied by much noisy chatter we were soon back on the road and onto the porridge. With one extra push, we found traction and resumed our journey once again.

We waltzed and skated through the porridge, almost to the Masaka township, the sight of which caused me to lift my eyes to heaven in gratitude. I had begun to hallucinate a large glass of ice-cold White Cap or Tusker lager, hovering just out of reach. The time was 5 pm. I had only eaten a few pieces of melon since my pastry at 11 am. The bananas I had seen were the hard bananas that the Africans grind up to make flour. My bum felt like a stranger to me and my shoulders felt as though they'd had the rack treatment in a torture chamber. I walked from the truck similar to how John Wayne walked from his horse after crossing the Grand Canyon.

Still, I hadn't let the side down and no doubt, 'One Man Went To Mow', or should I say, 'Dig', would be sung all over the Masaka district.

CHAPTER 13

It was now Thursday and the fourth day in Masaka. After my trip to Bukoba on Monday, I had assessed all that I needed to know regarding the Masaka office and township. One item at the top of the list was the old Albion truck, Grandma, which would be taken to the Kampala workshop for assessment. If feasible, it would have major surgery.

I completed my general maintenance survey earlier than expected but I didn't wish to return 'home'. Instead, I turned my attention to the external construction program. I found that there was a construction party doing a pole route diversion out in the Bundu, somewhere in the territory. Once again experiencing the first signs of itchy feet syndrome, I thought I might take a look at them. (The working party, not my feet.) Because I had a long way to go I took the small Chevrolet open truck and left dear old Grandma to the linesmen. It was small in comparison to Grandma but in much better condition. The 'Chevs' seemed to be quite popular in East Africa, especially so in Kenya.

When I eventually arrived in the area where the working party was supposed to be I had no problem finding them. They were making so much noise. They had dug a few deep holes for new poles to be erected and the holes were being inspected by the African foreman who was a great extrovert and massively vocal. He seemingly had everything and everybody under control.

Two or three of the holes had become occupied by snakes and the foreman took great delight in showing me how to solve the problem of ejecting them. Brimmed full of ego, he sallied forth, stood over the hole and dropped a piece of cloth or paper into the hole. Immediately the snake struck at the intrusion using its initial store of venom. Then, with a stick, he flicked the snake out of the hole. Not to be undertaken by a novice because there is a certain amount of expertise involved! One particular danger is that when the snake is being ejected out of the hole it may wrap itself around the stick and slide down on to the hand of the operator. Not always sure where the snake may land when it is flicked out willy-nilly into the air, it was not surprising that no one seemed to be too inquisitive, and no one wished to learn the noble art. They all kept well out of the way, including the Bwana!

I was told by the foreman that there was a team of European surveyors working only about thirty miles north which were probably working for the Ugandan government. Giving me this information was, I think, a splendid idea to get me out of the way. If that was the case, it worked. Naturally, being me, I decided to hunt them out for a chat. It would be a novelty to see another paleface!

It was extremely hot and humid. Nothing was on the road and there was just scrubland on either side. I was kicking up clouds of dust as I went in search of the surveying team. Just as I was beginning to wonder where they could be, I located a very sand-baked Land Rover by the side of the road and pulled up behind it. As I got out of the Chev, so did the occupier of the Land Rover.

We shook hands and introduced ourselves. Lol Parker was his name. He told me that the surveying work had been completed and that the rest of the party had returned to Kampala. He just wished to check a few things on foot and to verify various points before returning to Masaka before nightfall. He was a very keen photographer, almost an addict, (those were his words), and I could see that his camera was handy just in case there was an opportunity to use it.

I've always thought of surveyors as methodical men who are unhurried and always deep in thought. Lol was none of these. He was sharp, and a 'hurry-up' type of medium height. He was a little bony with a full head of hair, horn-rimmed glasses and had a near London accent. After we had discussed a few topics, I asked him how far he had to go for his 'on foot' check.

"Oh, just over the hillock," he said, pointing to a rise. I estimated it to be a few hundred yards away over dry scrubland with groups of trees dotted around.

"I'll come with you to keep you company," I said, "Stretching my legs will do me good". He was pleased with the offer of company, so off we went. Every now and again he would stop and take a few notes. There was a very reassuring thought that I would not get lost with a surveyor in tow.

I was still musing over this possibility when we both saw it. An elephant, not too close, and nothing to get alarmed about. They are not normally dangerous unless threatened, just like most animals. When threatened, of course, they are very dangerous and they are very big. Always follow the country code; 'Elephants have right of way'. There are also rogue elephants which are elephants that do not belong to a herd (due perhaps to rejection), and who have the reputation of being grumpy. I think understandably so!

This one appeared to be in the latter classification because there didn't seem to be any others in the vicinity. He started to head our way. How fast can they travel? Probably a lot faster than we can. Where to run and hide? We had passed a deep rut that was something similar to a golf bunker and I was thinking that it would be the ideal place. Then he made an awful noise as he became aware of us. "This way to the 'bunker', Lol", I said as we legged it!

The elephant was now definitely after us but fortunately, the bunker was nearer than I thought and we just fell into it. Old Grumpy was very noisy, which sent a chill down my spine. We kept huddled close to the side and bottom of the bunker and remained very still. Both of us petrified. I had come to believe that I was totally invincible because I had 'got away with it' in so many incidents previously but now wondered whether this really was my time to go. Yet, the longer the noise and ground stamping went on, the more I was gradually convinced that he had lost us and that I would survive.

He had lost us. He couldn't see us and was almost on top of us, floundering around for what seemed an awfully long time. Then he seemed to move away. I can't believe it to this day that as he did so, Lol moved quickly to put his head and shoulders above the bunker, took a snapshot of the elephant and then dropped down into the bunker again. Lunatic!!

The elephant came back to where it was before. He must have seen some movement. He was now almost on top of us. I just prayed that he wouldn't put his big feet into the bunker. One foot would be enough to send us to our maker. A few minutes later, which passed very, very slowly, the elephant went. He just walked away, probably having given up after not being able to see us. Thank the Lord!!

"Was it worth the risk, Lol?", I asked.

"No, it wasn't, Cy. So stupid of me. It's just instinct with me, and I apologise to you."

"Accepted," I said, "I'll have a print of it, Lol!!". We stayed for a respectable time in the bunker, looking out over the top to make sure the coast was clear before venturing out. I thought we would return to the vehicles after that episode but Lol had not finalised the exercise so further on we went.

"I just want to see what the elevation is on the other side of that craggy looking structure," said Lol, pointing. "Then we had better return." It was more bushy now with long clumps of bushes amongst the scrub.

I still had that funny gut feeling, perhaps because I wasn't in control of the situation. I was on the lookout for that damned elephant, continually casting my eyes over the terrain for means of a retreat to safety, just in case. Lol was a bit edgy and said that he would be glad to get back to the vehicles. Eventually, we arrived at his goal and Lol seemed satisfied and extremely happy to have done it. I was too. After the area had been inspected we turned and started on the return journey to our vehicles.

We were both keeping a wary eye on the surrounding ground, both being very concerned about Grumpy in case he decided to join us. I kept turning to look at the rear of us. That was the direction my 'sixth sense' was telling me the danger would come from. The landscape was also quite disorientating and one could easily get lost. I had an idea of the direction and Lol knew the direction, but our biggest fear was Old Grumpy.

I had just turned around once again after looking to our rear when suddenly a lion and four lionesses came out of the scrub about ten yards ahead of us. They were going from right to left across our path and then they all stopped!! My heart joined them! The piercing, very intent eyes of the lion will haunt me for the rest of my days. Yet, who was the biggest threat? The lion protecting his pride? Or the lionesses who were the hunters for food? There were FOUR lionesses. I hoped that they weren't hungry.

Anne's voice immediately entered my brain, "If you are ever threatened by a lion, never try to stare them out. Like the old adage, look slightly to the left of them, keeping them in sight, like any other cat would do if not seeking confrontation. That way you are not promoting a challenge".

I immediately did as she had told me to do and looked to the side of the lion's massive head. I concentrated on the very coarse hair on the side of his head below his ears. One false move or act to promote a threat, or turning and running (no matter how much temptation) would catapult the lions into attack mode. This stalemate continued for what seemed an age. I had witnessed it before in domestic cats. If Lol decided to act upon his instinct and go for a quick snap, we would be dead! Two or three huge bounds would be all that the lions needed. What a day! Any more confrontations and I would require new underpants.

'Make your mind up time' was lasting a gruelling long time on the part of the lions. God, was it never going to end? I felt curiously calm and would accept death if it should come. I thought of Anne and my family. Would Anne find out? How would my parents, brothers and sisters take the news? What a way to go! Was this what I had been saved for?

Then there was a movement. The lion's massive head slowly turned and looked away to his front in the direction that they had been walking. Dismissing us as no threat? But I could see at a glance that the lionesses were still staring at us and the second one was gazing very intently. I prayed that she had not been blessed with PMT. Then slowly, looking very reluctant, the lion moved off in the original direction. After what seemed an age, the lionesses turned their gaze and followed the lion as he slowly moved, turning their heads every now and then, just to make sure.

I couldn't believe it. I was actually trembling, probably with the thought of dying in such a barbaric, animalistic way. Then, the inquest!!

"I didn't think there were lions in this area, Cy, did you?", said Lol in a shaky voice. I agreed with him, also in a shaky voice.

"And another thing," I said. "They generally lie up during the heat of the day. Could the elephant have disturbed them?"

"God knows. I resisted the temptation to take a snap. I would have been shaking too much anyway!!". I was so pleased.

There was a nervous half-mile to get back to the vehicles. We accomplished this using all-around vision, yet still watching the ground for the odd snake that might be wishing for a confrontation, just to get in on the act.

Lol sent me an enlarged snap of Old Grumpy which I have always kept. Pity I didn't have one of the lions but I think that would have been pushing it a bit.

CHAPTER 14

Before I left Masaka, I went out of my way to completely confuse the linesmen by pointing to a dandelion flower and saying in Swahili, "Maradadi Simba". The literal translation is a beautiful, pretty, lovely or dandy lion. The linesmen had often confused me with some of their expressions so it was now their turn to be confused. Of course, there was no comprehension at all from them. They could see no connection whatsoever between a beautiful lion and a common flower. Also, in their eyes lions were not beautiful. All it did was to convince them that indeed I was a very funny Bwana who needed treatment.

I returned to Kampala from Masaka feeling like someone who has managed to escape the electric chair. I looked forward to a large slice of normality to compensate for my 'terror' confrontations.

Upon my arrival in Kampala Emily said that she had missed my presence at the flat, which I thought was nice of her to say. I didn't convey to her that due to circumstances beyond my control I could well have been permanently missed! She also surprised me by saying that she had been invited to a fancy dress party this Sunday in Mbuya and was asked to bring a friend. Would I care to accompany her?

I thought it so nice of her to consider me and not one of her doctor friends. I said, "It doesn't give us much time to get kitted up for a fancy dress party considering that it is now Friday does it, Emily?".

"Ah…. Well…" said Emily slowly, studying my face intently and looking at me with her bluish-grey eyes, all of a twinkle! "I've thought about that. We could go as two girls from St. Trinian's."

On hearing the last few words I quickly, cleverly and cunningly (or so

I thought) said, "What a pity, Emily. I am on emergency call on Sunday".

"Ah", replied Emily promptly. "Geoff, whose party it is, is in charge of forestry and has a telephone. So you can be reached there. Besides, Sunday should be quiet emergency-wise shouldn't it, Cy?" It doesn't look like I'm going to wriggle out of this!

Thinking quickly I said, "What about costumes at such short notice?". I was getting quite desperate now, hoping to derail this mad idea and I think she knew it.

"I've thought of that, Cy." She would have, of course! She was still staring at me intently trying to read my mind. I could also see that she was on the verge of breaking into a fit of the giggles. Her bottom lip was already quivering. All of which made me a little apprehensive as to what was coming next.

Still watching my face she said, "I have some big African nurses on my staff so I'm sure one of their uniforms, being of pinafore design, will fit you. We can fit two small cotton wool balls to your chest to give you a little bit of a figure". I couldn't believe what she was saying. She was looking away from me now. She had to, as her face mildly distorted while making a monumental effort to evade breaking into laughter. No wonder the doctors had not been invited. I know none of them would have remotely considered it.

Emily turned to look at me and at her first glance she cracked and lapsed into almost uncontrollable laughter. Pointing her finger at me she gasped, "Your face, Cy. A picture! I just can't help it". Dressed up like a big girl, eh? Imagining what we would look like as a pair and seeing Emily doubled up with laughter was enough. I burst into laughter with her.

On Saturday morning we went into the nurses' room at the hospital. All their uniforms were hung neatly on hooks along one side of the wall with tall, dark green lockers on the other side. Emily selected one garment for me and I proceeded to try it on. As I did so, two African nurses entered the room and uttered surprised, guttural noises as they espied me trying on the uniform. Their faces showed alarm, then relief when they noticed that Emily was present.

Trying to explain to the nurses what a fancy dress party is, was similar to naming the dandelion in Swahili to the African linesmen. Through African nurses' eyes, the Bwana and Mwana always dressed up nicely to go to parties. Why both of us should dress in nursing clothes was beyond comprehension. I thought of the Masaka linesmen hearing about me in my new outfit. It would be proof enough to them that I did indeed, need treatment.

I looked positively 'gorky' in the big, girly dress with it being a bit short in length. The fact that it was a pinafore dress and similar to a gymslip meant that I had no difficulty with the shoulder fitting. Emily was positively beaming and was on the cusp of giggling.

Emily came into my flat on the Sunday morning, all dressed for the occasion in what could be taken as a gymslip and blouse. I thought she looked quite erotically sexy but refrained from saying so in case I was verbally punished by her very able tongue. She helped me with my 'gear' and then pinned sisal extensions to the back of my hair to resemble ringlets. I feebly objected but to no avail. In nursing sister mode she said crisply, "We have to do it properly or not at all", as she deftly worked on my hair. The balls of cotton wool were fitted and other adjustments were made without resistance, knowing it would be futile to object. A bottle marked 'Gin' in big letters was attached to my waist and a homemade St. Trinian's Girls' School badge was attached to my chest.

I said, "You certainly have been working on this idea, plus all the details to sort out. What made you think that I would cooperate, Emily?".

"Cy," she said, "You are the only one I know who would be likely to take part after a little persuasion".

Titivating complete, we stood in front of the mirror. What a pair!! We looked just like some comedy stage act.

After I had sat in my new dress, walked around and generally got used to the feel of it, we had a coffee. Then, off we went in my car to Mbuya.

Emily was all cock-a-hoop and bubbly and I was trying desperately to familiarise myself with this new mode of dress, drive the car and to join her mentally.

Arriving at Mbuya we pulled up at Geoff's residence. It was a large old-worldly bungalow with cars parked all over the area. The ground was covered in sparse grass over volcanic rock. I could hear the chatter before I entered the driveway and it sounded as though it was going to be an interesting and happy party. Emily and I got out of the car and had a last-minute inspection of each other before we joined the melee.

Being introduced to Geoff was like being introduced to Howard Keele. Geoff was a broad-shouldered, big character complete with a small moustache. There was no fat!! He was just one hunk of a man (according to the ladies) with a deep Gloucestershire accent and a laugh which emitted from the basement. A nice, gentle giant, courteous and especially charming to the ladies. Although fifteen years more mature than I, it was natural that we hit it off at our first introduction. It was the beginning of a long friendship.

There was great hilarity when Emily and I entered the lounge. Everyone was so amused at our double act and I really felt like a big girl! The room looked set for a good party. There were such an array of costumes and characters, all intent on having fun. There were easily accessible drinks and a buffet laid out in the dining room.

Emily was really letting her hair down now. She had blossomed personality-wise and was actively taking part in the fun. So much so that I could hardly believe it was the same woman I had met on the train. Amongst all the noise I didn't hear the telephone. Geoff came to me as I was boisterously acting the fool with Emily. "You are wanted on the phone, Cy". The sentence stopped us in our tracks. Surely not an emergency on a Sunday afternoon. Surely not. The expression on Emily's face and the quick hand to her mouth showed her concern.

"This is the operator speaking, sir. There is a prompt red alarm for this building and there is a big noise and the building is shaking and I am frightened. Please come quickly, sir." Dressed like this??

I told Emily the reason for the call out and just as I was leaving I looked at her with a wan smile. She was covering her face with both hands, looking through her fingers to hide her amusement at my predicament. Yet, with a temporarily concerned look managed to mouth the words, "Sorry, Cy".

Big noise? One never knew what problem awaited on these call outs. Nothing that can't be solved of course, but a big noise?

Sunday afternoon was dressing up time for the Asian community. They congregated near the Communications Building which was situated near a big, colourful roundabout covered in flowers, with a park on the opposite side. There were ladies in beautiful coloured sarees and dresses and men in Sunday best strolling and sitting around the area. The youngsters were clean and polished and were running and playing. Sunday is a day set aside for a family ritual which included grandparents, uncles and aunts, and all the attendant children, all seemingly very content.

I had great respect for the whole Asian community. They were very industrious and hard-working; the backbone of the economy. Almost all the dukas (shops) were Asian-owned. In my everyday activities at work, shopping, groceries etc., I had many Asian friends. All were so well mannered and polite with a ready sense of humour and were so easy to get on with. I had a special relationship with a Goan family by the name of Sequeira. I think of them often and would love to know how they are today.

I arrived at the communications HQ and stopped the car. I could certainly hear the noise. There were groups of Asians around the place, which had become a focal point because of the noise emanating from it. Another group were across the road, all concerned and drawn to this particular strange thumping noise.

It was into this very inquisitive crowd that I stepped out of the car. I could feel the intensive gaze from all gathered there. A sudden and complete silence descended from all the Sunday chatter, as I, a big, freakish 'girl' walked across the wide pavement in a pinafore dress with funny hair ringlets and man shoes. I unlocked the door. Then, most probably due to the gin and tonic effect, I just had to turn around and wave to them before going inside. Now they really had something worthwhile to discuss on this quiet Sunday afternoon!

I first went up to the top floor to calm the telephone operator down and assured him the loud noise would not hurt him. Then, downstairs to confront the problem coming from the Power Room. The very large, automatic, diesel standby engine (a lovely black shiny monster) covered half the room's width. It was designed to automatically take over the power supply in the event of a disruption in the mains power supply. Today, however, it was making an almighty racket. The noise inside the power room was horrendous and reverberated throughout the whole building. The reason for the noise was that the engine was starting up and then releasing. It would not hold in or shut down.

At the far end of the Power Room was the power control panel which was a free-standing structure fixed to the floor away from the wall (for easy access to the rear). Approximately eight feet tall, it occupied three-quarters of the wall area at the far end and was made of a thick, shiny black Ebonite type of material. It was always kept in immaculate condition, as were the generators and all the other equipment. Access to the Power Room was restricted to Senior Engineers.

The sizeable circuit breakers with insulated spring-loaded stirrup handles (designed to accommodate large hands) occupied the main part of the left side of the panel. The circuit breakers would automatically 'crash out', triggering the alarm lights and bells if a loss of mains power (or another major fault) occurred. Also on the panel were large-faced voltmeters, manual rheostats (to adjust voltage levels on restarting), plus other controls for isolating and changing over the switches.

The circuit I was interested in on this occasion had three large, knife-edged, lever-type switches approximately eighteen inches long with black insulated handles representing the three phases of the mains supply. On disconnecting these from the mains supply, the diesel engine relinquished its hiccups and began to run smoothly and continuously. The fault was due to a one-phase power supply failure. Once restored I reset and closed the engine down. Restarting the four foot long generator, adjusting the voltage and closing the circuit breakers completed the procedure. If it had been a 'normal' three-phase failure there would have been less of a problem.

I thought the crowd would have diminished when I came out, but oh no!! The word had got around about the strange happenings at the building and the crowds had grown much larger. On sallying forth from the building the crowd went quiet once again, staring at the apparition walking to the car. Apart from those who knew about the European madness of a fancy dress party and were laughing, the remainder once again were staring fascinated.

Just before I got into the car someone started clapping and soon they were all clapping. I acknowledged them with a wave, feeling like the star in a Sunday afternoon matinee. Why the applause? Was it for my theatrical performance and the entertainment I had provided? My costume? Or the fact that I had stopped the noise? I would love to know.

CHAPTER 15

One evening I was called out to an emergency. It was an evening that Emily and I had arranged to play Canasta in her flat. We often played Canasta, and I appreciated the fact that she was such good company. She was self-disciplined and so well organised, similar to me. Beneath the prim and proper nursing sister veneer was a quick-witted and fun personality. Although the quick (and sometimes caustic) wit was always hovering ready to be deployed, the fun aspect seemed somewhat curtailed. I think she must have used a whole year's ration at Geoff's fancy dress party.

Due to the emergency call out I was fifteen-minutes late arriving at her flat. Upon entering, I apologised for my late arrival and said, "I had a call out, Emily. Still, better late than never", in my usual happy tone. Emily came back with, "Better late than never? Better never late!!", in her best nursing sister voice. What an attitude! I grinned inwardly. There were no sympathetic utterances regarding my call out. I wondered what fate would await any little African nurse who arrived late for duty. It doesn't bear thinking about. I should imagine that all the oxygen bottles were at attention and bedpans facing the correct way, in her hospital.

In the flat, I noted the usual small extra table. The contents on the surface were goodies to be eaten later but were currently covered and protected by a light linen cloth. A bottle of whiskey, two glasses, Canada Dry ginger ale and playing cards were placed on the adjacent table which had two chairs pulled out ready for us to sit down. Everything in its place.

During the game, Emily said, "I hope to visit friends in Nakuru soon and must book a compartment on the train. I absorbed this information and after giving it some thought said, "I'll be going to see Roy Smith soon. He is stationed near Eldoret. Perhaps we can arrange a date so that we can go together in the car. I don't mind going the extra 100 miles because I would love to drive over Timboroa at 9,000 feet in daylight. I will be able to visit Roy on the return journey". Emily readily accepted the invitation. I remembered how scared she had been going over Timboroa in the train. Although I referred to Roy staying at Eldoret, he was actually living further south at Kakamega on the Kakamega – Busia road. Eldoret was the nearest town.

Emily and I agreed a date to travel and it was arranged for me to stay at Nakuru for a night or two with Emily and her friends, who had ample accommodation. In the meantime, Abdul suggested that I attend my final examination. "I know it is a little premature but I think you are ready to cope," he said, "Besides, if you fail it will give you some idea as to the standard you would have to achieve next time".

So the date was set and I attended. Just Abdul, and Abdul's lookalike were the examiners. They greeted me with broad, friendly smiles in an informal setting. Abdul set the ball rolling.

"Fully describe your journey, in Swahili, from when you left your house in England until you arrived at Nairobi airport". This is not going to be a pushover! Nobody would be able to accuse Abdul of going easy on his pupils!

I tarried awhile to collect my thoughts before plunging in. To impress the examiners I mentioned small details and hoped it would make a good impression (which it did, according to Abdul, later). I duly completed the task which was quite a marathon, yet I felt confident with what I had described. 'I wonder if I have passed it', I mused.

"Describe your work. What you do. And some of the equipment you encounter during the day." God! It's not finished. That was Abdul's lookalike asking his question.

Electronic equipment and associated moving parts were a no-go area because there are no Swahili-equivalent words. But I did attempt to do so with the power equipment, which I think made a good impression judging by their raised eyebrows and shallow smiles. I described a generator as 'mashini kwa nguvu kwa umeme', which meant 'machine with the power of lightning'. There was no Swahili term for electricity then. The problem was that the most frequent cause of faults to stop the generators from working was caused by 'nguvu kwaumeme' (lightning), which taken literally was also the motivating power. They were both laughing now and stopped me at this juncture, coming across to shake my hand and were very amused.

"You have passed your final Swahili examination," both were still beaming at me, "And there is to be no written examination".

I felt elated that I had now passed the Swahili barrier. Abdul was highly delighted also, and repeated, "I knew you could do it". I thanked him for his tuition and asked him to pass on the good news and my greetings to his cousin Abdul in Nairobi. There was nothing to stop me now, unless I was a very naughty boy.

Whilst at Geoff's fancy dress party I met Alf and Bert who were two middle-aged men from Lancashire. They were set like concrete in their ways, having been born with broad Lancs accents that were honed to perfection with much usage. Bert who was stocky, blunt and adamant with a loud, deep voice, claimed to have better knowledge than various experts in their fields. He was easy to tease about his attitude, accepting, when pressed very hard by me, that he was indeed talking a load of bull.

Alf was much taller, of thinner construction and had a quiet voice, occasionally managing to complete a whole sentence before his words were obliterated by Bert. I referred to them as Sandbag and Lamppost, a wartime image.

Their work entailed installing complex machinery in a new cotton mill at Jinja. They had been "Put up in this 'ere 'otel" in Jinja and did not like it because they were unaccustomed to hotel life. Home cooking was sadly missed. "It's not like 'ome", said Alf.

At the party, feeling very benevolent and a little sorry for them I offered them my flat to stay in, if I decided to leave it for any length of time. They seemed grateful at such an offer. So when the date of our safari to Nakuru was finalized I invited them for drinks and showed them around the flat, where they would be staying for four weeks. They were highly delighted when they arrived at my flat on the morning of our departure to Nakuru.

Emily once again, Miss Organised as ever, had refreshments and incidentals for our journey with nothing forgotten. When we left Kololo Hill we called at Nakasero Hospital because Emily wished to make a call there. Thence, we went down to the roundabout with much floral colour, past the Imperial Hotel and the Communications Building on our right and the Standard Bank of South Africa on our left. We then turned left on to Kampala High Street, passing Barclays on our right and The City Bar on our left, where succulent steaks were to be had. It was a very popular venue for both casual lunchtimes and formal evening meals. We carried on past the Old Port Bell and Mbyua Road junction on our right, and then left Kampala for Jinja, 50 miles away.

Out on the Jinja Road, which was tarmac and recently constructed, we passed through the Mabira Forest. During the road construction and the initial few weeks after opening, there was fierce opposition from the baboons and rumour has it that rocks and stones were thrown at passing vehicles. Apart from baboons there were many other 'monkey types', namely the Colobus monkeys and Red-tailed monkeys with plenty of leopards for them to worry about. The tarmacked road seemed unreal after bush roads and with its straight lines, looked as though it had been carved out of the forest with a sharp knife.

On approaching Jinja, the Owen Falls Dam looked majestic in ivory white stone, having been recently constructed. It was 1954 and the dam was about to be commissioned to supply electric power to Uganda and part of Kenya. There had been very little opposition to its construction which was soon overcome when the enormous benefit to the territories was realised.

The main reason I wished to stop at Jinja was to stand on the spot where John Hanning Speke stood in 1862 when he discovered the source of the Nile. He named the lake, Victoria (after Queen Victoria) and it is at this point that the Nile, the longest river in the world, commences its journey from the largest African lake. It is also the second largest fresh water lake in the world. The actual point where the lake flows outwards to become the Nile is, or was, known as Ripon Falls after the Marquess of Ripon, a former president of the Royal Geographical Society. Owen's Falls was named after Major R Owen, a member of Sir Gerald Portal's 1893 expedition to Uganda.

Whilst in 'naming mode' you may be interested to know how Jinja acquired its name. 'Ejjinja' in Luganda language means 'stones' and in the vicinity of Owen's Falls is, or was, a memorial tribal stone. Ejjinja has most probably been honed to the present day Jinja by European influence.

I stood by the falls where Speke must have stood and tried to imagine how he must have felt as he stood there, looking at the start of the Nile, which would take three months to eventually flow into the Mediterranean. It must have been an emotional experience after years of searching, danger and hardship. He must have felt so excited to discover this elusive site, relieved for a mission accomplished and so proud to be an Englishman and making such a discovery.

His name is engraved on a large plaque which lays flat on the ground, which I was privileged to see and to stand on. I have heard that Ripon Falls and the plaque are now buried beneath the water due to the operation of the Owen Falls Dam. But I believe that another plaque has been erected at the site for future generations to see. The beautiful Bujagali Falls (which I thought was more like a series of rapids) are eight kilometres downstream and have not been adversely affected by the operation of the dam.

Reluctantly we left Jinja and pushed on through Bugiri and through Tororo township on a typical bush road. Passing on our right, Tororo

Rock measured approximately 5,000 feet high. It had been in our sights for miles. I believe it to be of volcanic construction but it does not have a great crater. A few miles later we were over the border and into Kenya, stopping occasionally to see Africa.

On the first stop I dutifully reconnoitred the ground to find a suitable and safe spot for Emily. This was a gentleman's privilege and the norm in Uganda. I then stood at a respectable distance.

On this occasion Emily came from behind a bush with her knickers dangling from her hand. "I've wet them, Cy", she said, in a very forceful voice with eyes which conveyed the message, 'Laugh, and you are dead'. I had turned my head away to hide the amused expression on my face. She looked so outraged.

"Bringing back childhood memories, Emily? I thought you wouldn't be wearing any". I was not being facetious. With it being so hot and humid in Uganda the majority of women went knickerless.

"I thought I had better wear them, travelling to cool Kenya." Laughing she said, "Obviously, I had better practice wearing them again. I'll get another pair out of my bag".

"I would wait until it really cools down, Emily. It will save turning your bag upside down". Then, tongue in cheek, "I won't take advantage of the situation".

"I'm not unduly perturbed, Cy. With these roads your hands are well and truly occupied." There was no such thing as power assisted steering then.

Mmm!! Sometimes I wondered about Emily! But not for long. She would most certainly revert into nursing sister mode if and when the occasion demanded it.

I must say at this juncture that the modesty of knickerless women in Uganda can be threatened by 'Dust Devils'. They are miniature whirlwinds or tornadoes, up to one foot high that can travel around at high speed, even on Kampala High Street. A Dust Devil drags and dissipates dust as it twists its way forward, hence the name Dust Devils. On one occasion a lady was walking towards me near the Crested Crane Café on Kampala High Street when a Dust Devil came from behind her. It lifted her Tootal cotton skirt up to her face, albeit only momentarily, due to her instant reaction and the sheer speed of the Dust Devil which made the experience short-lived. The initial panicked expression on her face was soon followed by knowing smiles of a secret shared as we passed each other. Emily's expression of 'It pays to advertise' sprung to mind.

After leaving Uganda the roads became progressively drier and dustier. The lush green of Uganda gave way to paler vegetation the higher we went as we climbed towards Eldoret. We had only met a couple of fellow travellers en route since leaving Jinja. At one point (I think near Webuye), we forded a river with fingers crossed and then went straight into a violent electrical storm with heavy rain coming down like walking sticks. The road became a sea of porridge and we came very near to being bogged down on quite a few occasions. We only just managed to keep the revs up and weaved our way through it, but through it we went and eventually arrived at Eldoret.

Eldoret seemed quite high up but after leaving there (in a hurry), it was another steady climb until we reached Timboroa at 9,000 feet where we were enclosed by mountain peaks. The air was much fresher, but being daytime was not as cold as it was on the train journey. We noticed the effects of the higher altitude. One such effect is due to the rarefied air. Never use the choke on starting the engine otherwise great difficulty will be had getting the engine to run.

After a suitable rest we quite happily continued downhill on the last leg of our journey and eventually arrived at Nakuru, just as the light was fading. Emily's friends lived just outside Nakuru in a beautifully constructed abode. There were detached timber huts that were furnished for guests situated around a very large courtyard. The larger main residence (the owner's quarters) also had a communal dining room and lounge, with 'help yourself' drinks.

Ada and Charles, who owned the property, were extremely hospitable (being Kenya types, of course). Friends with companions who just dropped in were made very welcome. There was always a room and a bed with food and drinks, lavishly bestowed on a tired traveller. I was very impressed. I knew such lovely people existed, but I had never met any of them until now.

A log fire was lit in the evening with Nakuru being still quite high up and distinctly cooler than Uganda. There was much bon ami and the hosts participated in a good, vocal evening. Both Emily and I plus the others present were drawn to the fire. Due to the journey, such ample good food and drinks and now the fire, yawns gradually became more frequent. A late night was not to be. Emily toddled off first, then one after another the remainder of the guests peeled off to their respective quarters. I ended up hitting the sack at quite a reasonable time.

I slept like a baby until pigeons, making their usual cooing awoke me. In the room the ablution arrangements were primitive (in comparison to 'in town' toilet facilities), yet adequate. The water tap was covered by a muslin cloth to filter off any sizable debris and insects that had managed to enter the rainwater tank on the roof.

Breakfast was a come-and-go occasion with no set time. Emily arrived a little later than I did, both of us having slept well. As she sat down to breakfast, prim, proper and orderly, I whispered to her, "Are you dry?". I received a most withering look, with her lips tightly sealed. I gleefully ate my breakfast.

I pottered about during the day chatting to Emily and the other guests, trying to find out if there was a passable road through to Narok. Because, once through Narok, going down the escarpment would hopefully see me through to the Maasai Mara National Reserve. I thought that I might as well see as much as I can whilst I am in the area.

Charles was very helpful, "Swap vehicles, Cy. You may need the Land Rover. It's a tricky road from all accounts and I wouldn't try it if I were you. Still, if you wish to, Ada and I are going to Naivasha tomorrow, on tarmac. We can take your car". Brilliant!! I thanked him and set about rearranging vehicles.

As I pulled Emily's chair out for her at breakfast the next morning she looked up into my face and said, "I am dry and you are a pig". "Thank you, Emily", I said. She didn't want me to go to Narok.

"It's not a recognised route, Cy. I'm going to relax today, write some letters and catch up on some lost time with Ada when she returns from Naivasha. Why don't you stay too instead of gallivanting off the beaten track?" I'm sure she knew full well that the request was a lost cause.

Emily walked with me to the Land Rover, chatting. Just before boarding she gave me a hug and kissed me on the cheek which was not at all like Emily. Driving out of the courtyard I was confused once again. Should I have stayed? It's not like Emily to be so demonstrative. Women? Was it another Jodie and iron situation? And there was no headache!! Was I reading Emily wrong? No, I think not! She was perhaps a little worried about my trip. After all, we were very good friends and understood each other. Down boy! Get back to your kennel.

Out on the road I took my mind off my recent puzzle by singing at the top of my voice. I really enjoyed myself. The Land Rover bounced around on the corrugations. It was so different to other vehicles with the suspension being so hard, but I should imagine it to be ideal and come into its own in wet conditions. Narok, here I come!

I had only gone a few more miles when I became distinctly queasy. I felt clammy and quite nauseous. Surely my singing was not that bad. Beginning to feel worse I stopped the Land Rover to get out and looked carefully around me. Everywhere was deep scrub with the odd boulder. I wondered what might be concealed in there. It was unnatural. Very quiet without the slightest noise. In fact, unreal. In the distance were storm clouds.

Suddenly, I was violently sick. Repeatedly and rapidly retching I went down on my knees and stayed there for a while expecting that the sickness would go. But no, it started again. Then it started to rain. Heavy rain became heavier with thunder and lightning. I was retching almost continuously. It had all started so suddenly. It then started at the 'other end'. I quickly took off my shorts. I felt dreadful. I had taken my shorts off just in time and they were lying on some twiggy growth.

The situation was becoming quite serious. My bush shirt stuck to me with sweat and heavy rain. During a slight pause in my vomiting, I dismally thought how vulnerable I was to anything wanting sustenance. I felt so wretched. The rain was exceptionally heavy. Muddy water was running around my knees like a miniature river with leaf fragments floating downstream, catching my knees and moving on. It's strange how these moments are printed on your mind, never to be forgotten.

After a while I stopped being sick. Holding onto the vehicle I struggled to get up. I was filthy. I managed to clean my nether regions with the safari facilities that were always carried in vehicles. Just this effort exhausted me. I stood for a while unable to pull on my soaked shorts. They were so wet and heavy that they stuck to my body. I hadn't the strength, so I stood leaning against the Land Rover as the rain lashed down on me. My legs were weak and wobbly. I took some deep breaths, sipped some water and began to recover.

Eventually, I pulled on my shorts but initially couldn't fasten them. The energy had gone from my fingers. I had a nasty headache, but thank God, the sickness had subsided. More importantly the 'other end' was okay but still on fire. I struggled into the Land Rover and sat down very gingerly in my soaking wet shorts. The storm was abating and I could see the sun reappearing.

I must have been stranded for one or two hours, yet thankful that I could sit and rest. I felt more secure being inside the Land Rover. My right arm was resting on the door with the window open and I was so glad the sickness was over. I glanced at my arm and it was pale green. Noticing this had a marked effect on me and I fell out of the truck to be sick once again. The thought passed my mind that if I didn't make it back they did know which road I was on, but nobody else would come this way. Only the odd person and silly sods like me.

I was beginning to feel sorry for myself and wished that I had taken Emily's advice in having a relaxing day. Sipping water to help my fluid level, I knew that I had to be patient and hope time would bring my strength back. I managed to drag myself back into the Land Rover once again but it took even more effort than the last time. Feeling wretched, wet through and shivering, I closed my eyes. I immediately went dizzy so quickly reopened them.

With a sudden fit of determination to get back, I started the engine. It gave me something else to focus on instead of my condition. Slowly I turned the vehicle around and moved forward. The road had now turned into porridge due to the storm. Thank goodness for the Land Rover! For safety's sake I kept it in first gear for a long spell, then into second gear slowly going back to Nakuru. I fought to overcome the desire to stop and succumb. Keeping on the road was taking all my strength but on and on I went. God, it seemed an eternity, until with utter relief I saw the entrance. Feeling near death's door, I trundled into the courtyard, stopped the engine and pressed the horn. Frank, a resident came out with two African staff. Then, through a haze I saw Emily. There was consternation on her face as she immediately took charge. I gave up then. Emily, thank God! She'll sort me out.

I was put into a heavenly warm bath by Frank and Emily. Emily applying a soft sponge over my body. Modesty had gone for a walk and I didn't care. I kept drifting off but remembered being assisted out of the luxurious bath where I really wanted to stay.

I awoke with Emily standing at the bed taking my pulse. She leant down and kissed me on the cheek. "You'll live, Cy", she whispered. It seemed so dark and cramped. Another bed was touching the one I was in. I saw a large alarm clock with fluorescent face showing 3:15 am, then I fell asleep again.

It was mid-morning when I awoke with Emily opening the door, the bright sun behind her. She came and sat on the bed. "You've had a rough time, Cy, haven't you? But you are looking much better now".

"Where the hell am I, Emily?"

"You are in my room at Charles and Ada's place. I had another bed put in here so that I could keep an eye on you". Then with a mischievous cheeky grin, added, "Don't get any ideas that it could be permanent". My brain could not afford the effort to master her last remark.

She went over to a cabinet and came back with a basin and mouthwash. She used a flannel on my hands and face. Later she said, "Hungry yet?".

"Yes, Emily, I do believe I am."

"Good," she said, "Don't expect anything too great to start with". And off she went, out of the door.

A little while later she came back with a bowl of soup and a spoon and tucked a towel around my chest. I managed three-quarters of it but my arms were so tired. She came over and spoon-fed the rest to me and looked happy that I'd had something to eat. Frank, Charles and Ada visited me before I dropped off to sleep.

During the afternoon I got up and shuffled around the room feeling light-headed. Emily made the bed, to which I returned, waking up in the evening. She went out once again and came back with a meal of minced chicken in a milky, saucy concoction. I felt much better after I had consumed it. Emily came and sat on the bed. We talked for a while. I noticed a look of tenderness in her eyes which I had never seen before. I wondered what had happened to nursing sister mode when with another mischievous facial expression, she said, "If you promise to behave yourself, you can stay another night".

"Don't go tempting me then, it could kill me". And genuinely thought that it probably would.

CHAPTER 16

Although I had made a complete recovery I was loath to leave the excellent company at Nakuru, Emily in particular. We had become such good friends. The companionship with Emily was easy-going. We understood each other, especially after my recent sickness and the loving, professional care given by Emily had bonded our friendship. I sensed she felt the same when I received a kiss and a long hug from her before entering my car. Purely platonic, nothing suggestive from 'Our Emily'. Yet, I was always optimistic that it could be otherwise. She looked deceivingly like a lonely figure when I looked back to wave from the car on leaving the courtyard. Consequently, due to all the accumulative delays, I started my journey later than I intended.

I climbed the few miles up to Nakuru and then once I was through the town, I headed out on to the Londiani – Kisumu Road. I had thought of going further south via Kericho and the plantations but had to abort the idea. I could not see me making it to Roy's before nightfall and I did not want to pussyfoot around Kakamega looking for him in the dark. There were no mobile phones then so I made Kisumu my objective for an overnight stay.

After passing through Londiani it was downhill to Kisumu. The vegetation gradually became thicker and greener. I was enjoying myself singing as I travelled, and I loved driving, especially so in Africa with all the road free and the excitement of not knowing what may lie ahead. I was making good progress, travelling at approximately 50 mph with dust clouds billowing behind me and scrub hedge either side. Suddenly from left to right hurtled a load of deer and African cattle! It seemed like a mixture of animals to me and I was right in amongst them. It was over so quickly and I was amazed that none of the animals had collided with me. I stopped the car, jumped out and was about to investigate when second thoughts had me jumping back in again, with great alacrity.

It would have made a good scene in a film. What had spooked them? Were there any great big pussy cats chasing them? If so, out of the car in the middle of the road I would be ideally placed for a good mauling. The thought of which petrified me, triggering memories of Lol and I and our confrontation with Leo and his wives. I stayed a while, but nothing happened.

Whilst I was stationary I realised that I was missing Emily's company. She was such a good conversationalist with her cryptic remarks and funny quips. It made me wonder whether I could have made a supreme effort during my lapse in good health to advance from first base in my relationship with her. Ever the optimist! Perhaps not so far as to stop her falling out of bed. That would, I'm sure, have sent me to my maker, in my state of health at that time. No! Something a little subtler maybe, just to test the ground. It made me cringe just thinking about it and it would be a long-lost hope knowing Emily. An outraged Emily armed with a lethal 'Emily vocal broadside' ranged directly at me would surely have brought out that hidden yellow streak in me.

I must stress here that I am not on my own. During the war I witnessed burly, brave men show massive yellow streaks. They would guiltily cringe in fear when a stout, big-bosomed matron appeared at the hospital entrance pinpointing illegal smokers with an eagle eye. So be it.

Looking out through the car window I resisted the temptation to get out and have a look around outside, probably due to the thought of self-preservation more than anything else. I just started the car and carried on to Kisumu. I don't remember very much about Kisumu. It was a pleasant little town with a small, comfortable hotel. I had a good night's sleep and breakfast, then I was out on the Kakamega road. I call it a road but it was more like a dried-up river bed. It was full of boulders, assorted rocks of different dimensions, stones and shale. I just had to take a photograph of the road, yet the picture does not reflect the size of the stones or portray the way I felt negotiating it. I arrived at Kakamega after travelling approximately 50 km and stopped to examine my tyres. Amazingly no problems.

I found Roy's place quite easily. It was simple enough in daylight. The majority of properties had name boards at the entrance. I turned into the drive and there was Smithy with his usual cocky, yet laconic smile, which said it all. It was arranged that during my visit, we would de-coke his car, which is not a usual task nowadays, but essential then.

The next day we had the cylinder head off the engine and made good progress grinding the valves in etc. We spent our evenings recapturing events in Nairobi and Africa, yet always ending up with a laugh and witty end remark from one of us. And we couldn't forget to drink to everyone's health, of course!

A few nights into my stay I was suddenly awakened from a deep sleep by a most terrible, fearful noise. I was out of bed so fast and met Roy tumbling out of his bed. The noise was a dreadful animal noise outside. Suffice to say we did not have any desire to investigate. Then, it abruptly stopped. We looked at each other trying to put a meaning to the noise. Both of us had been in a deep sleep. Smithy looked as though he had too. We decided to return to our beds, accepting the fact that some animal disagreement had taken place.

The houseboy awoke us the next morning. He was quite excited and beckoned for us to come and look outside. A dead leopard laid just by the drive. Its head had the most terrible of injuries and the houseboy showed us that its neck was broken. A lion and leopard fight had taken place, and the houseboy animatedly demonstrated how the lion had hit the leopard's head with its paw. Having seen the size of a lion's paw and its massive strength, I didn't doubt it! It wasn't very pleasant to see at breakfast time and I really felt sorry for the leopard. Smithy had mentioned there were quite a few snakes around but had not mentioned anything about our feline friends. When I prodded him about lions he quite casually said, "Well, Cy, I must admit I have heard quite a few grunts since moving in". Then, tongue in cheek, as is often the case with Smithy, he said, "I knew you had a 'thing' about lions, so I thought I wouldn't mention it".

It was an easy-going friendship, always casual and humorous but we both knew that when the chips were down we would and could rely on the other completely. Now that we had completed the work on the car, I was looking forward to the rest of the time there, but it was never to be.

After breakfast one morning I suddenly went dizzy and hot so went outside and sat down. My back was aching which was foreign to me. I just did not suffer from backache. After one hour, after having shown no improvement, Roy said, "It's obvious you've got a temperature, Cy. There is nothing in the way of medication here. The nearest medic is in Eldoret".

I thought to myself that being ill must not become a habit as it's spoiling my lifestyle. If I had picked up something nasty the best course of action would be to hightail it back to Kampala whilst the fever is in the early stages and whilst it is still quite early in the day.

Roy agreed after a little thought and said, "It's going to be a tough one if the fever develops — which it most probably will. But I can see your point. You might easily get quite a long way towards home in the same time as it would take to Eldoret. There is no short cut through to Eldoret". The Kakamega forest was not an option.

"If I decide to go for Kampala, Roy, what's the backroad like through Mumias and on to Busia? It will save me a lot of time compared to going back south to Kisumu, especially on that God-forsaken dried-up river bed called a road!!"

"Well, it's a bit wriggly down to Mumias but better after Mambare to Busia." Then, with a cheeky grin, "But it can be naughty when wet".

Decision time again!!

I said, "Okay, I'll take it. If I feel I can't make it at Busia, I can always go up to Tororo. Then there is Jinja I can fall to!!".

I sat down by the bed packing my few things and had a little rethink. It's going to be no picnic getting back. I thought about Smithy. It was such a shame I had to leave. I also thought about his remarks earlier. He had a way with his expressions. "I knew you had a 'thing' about lions", he had said. A 'thing'? Cheeky sod! A typical Smithy utterance. Yes, you are damn right, I do have a 'thing' about lions. And if you had mentioned it earlier I would not have had any desire to bend over looking into your car engine with my backside beautifully stretched waiting for a rogue Leo to pat!

CHAPTER 17

Roy and I exchanged a strong handshake with a mutual understanding, then I was gone. He was right about a wriggly road. It was also damp and slippery. Great care was needed. Yet, even though I felt light-headed and unnaturally hot, I was well in control. Kampala was in my sights and I was determined to get there. After passing Mumias the wriggly road straightened out somewhat and I felt relieved that I had passed through the expected rough part whilst I was reasonably able to do so.

Surprisingly, I was making good headway and travelling as fast as I dared in my condition, but I did notice a gradual deterioration both in my vision and general condition. Just past Mumias I almost got bogged down on a bad stretch of muddy road. It took a lot out of me, strength-wise, to negotiate my way through it. Worse was to come between Mambere and Busia when I suddenly ground to a halt, bogged down in porridge. I had been hoping to reach Busia and be rid of this backroad. Only a few miles and I would have been there.

Resting my head on the steering wheel trying to think my way out of this one, I could feel the sweat on my forehead and the increased heat, now that I had stopped. I heard a slight noise and turning my head, I looked into the face of an African woman peering at me through the open window of my door. Immediately she called out and seconds later African men surrounded the car. Friendly? Rapid talking ensued between them. I picked up the woman's words, "Bwana mgonjwa", (Bwana sick). Then a very excited cry from the passenger side window ,"Nyoka, nyoka!", (Snake, snake!). I was trying to take this in when I saw it. A snake was in front of the passenger seat, poking its head out from beneath a towel and a rolled up shirt (plus the other odds and ends on the floor of the car).

Almost immediately the door opened and a forked stick was thrust over the snake just behind its head, then removed expertly by one of my visitors whilst shouting, "Mtoto, mtoto" (Baby), referring to the snake. To me it had looked at least a teenager. It was black and most probably a Mamba, so very dangerous, even in its youth. I just prayed that 'mother' wasn't here also. I must have been ill to allow that to take up residence, not daring to think of how long it had been there keeping me company. It didn't talk like Emily, so I wasn't aware of it. It most probably boarded at Roy's place.

The Africans, meanwhile, were hacking small branches from the scrub and putting them under the wheels of the car. Different members of the tribe kept coming to the window smiling and conversing with me in Swahili, "Mzuri Bwana", (all is well), and, "Bwana mgonjwa", (Bwana sick). They tapped their foreheads where perspiration was gathering on mine. Then shouting, "Kwenda Bwana, kwenda sasa!", (Go Bwana, go now), and with the usual cheerleader, the car was propelled out of the pit of porridge. They ran alongside me waving and noisily gesturing to me to keep going. They did this until I got on to firmer ground and I, remembering my good manners, repeatedly sounded the horn to show my gratitude.

After a few more miles I was at Busia and the Uganda border which is about 110 miles to Kampala. Mmm! At this point, I very much doubted that I would make it. I wondered what I was suffering from. Tick typhus? Malaria? I was drinking loads of water and seeing Africa as a consequence. Now, as well as my rising body heat, I had the Uganda climate to contend with and my head felt as though it was floating on my neck.

As I approached Jinja I knew that it would take all my strength and determination to cover the last 50 miles to Kampala. Should I divert to Jinja or risk collapsing before reaching Kampala? Decision time once again. Pros and cons. Positives and negatives. The most influential aspect was the tarmac road beyond Jinja, meaning no fighting with the steering wheel and consequently, no drain on my reserves of strength. So, through Jinja onto the tarmac road I went, hell-bent for Kampala.

Nearing the end of the journey I felt strangely elated. I thought 'I'll make it now for sure', as I went into Kampala by the 'back door road', turning right before the township, then up Kololo Hill, and eventually pulling up outside the flat. I was home, I'd made it! Staring at the flat I had very mixed emotions. Yes, I had done it. Yes. But there was no Emily next door. It won't be the same without Emily and I felt terrible.

The Lancashire lads, Bert and Alfie were very surprised to see me and very alarmed by my condition. I was quickly taken to the hospital to see Bob, Dr Bob Milne, who was the duty doctor. It was soon diagnosed that I had malaria. How the hell had I contracted malaria? As far as I could remember I had always taken my prophylactic.

To my surprise, Bob didn't return my friendly smile. Far from receiving a friendly and sympathetic bedside manner from him, it soon became obvious that he was definitely anti-Cy!

"You wouldn't have contracted malaria if you had been taking your prophylactic! It almost amounts to your malaria being self-inflicted! I think you have been both forgetful and very stupid.

"Just one pill each week would have prevented this. Now you must suffer the consequences. We will get you home to bed. There is no special, magical medication. It won't be pleasant, especially when it really kicks in. After it has peaked, all being well, you should be okay. It is a very dangerous disease, and preventable, except for the forgetful. I just hope and pray that you will come through it okay! Emily will be very annoyed with you when she returns."

Cor, what a broadside. Except for the forgetful? What a sarcy and antagonistic Sod! What happened to the, "Have a G&T, Cy"? It would have been a much more companionable attitude. Where was the friendly Bob of yesterday?

Lying on top of the hospital bed I was already feeling at an all-time low. Rock bottom, in fact. Hot one minute, shivering with cold the next. I felt that Bob had kicked me down a mineshaft. He expected me to slither off home on my belly, grovelling for forgiveness yet far from being admonished. I became quite militant, but only in my own mind (as I didn't hold any cards). Who the hell does he think he is? I'll tell Emily about this when she comes home. Perhaps I will be able to persuade her to give him a workover with a typical Emily verbal tirade. Haha! That will sort him out.

I felt mirthful in my deranged state and was giggling away whilst being watched by two Africans orderlies with puzzled expressions. I would have felt better but for the damned malaria which was playing havoc with my thought process. Yes, thinking was becoming disjointed. Forgetful? Sod Bob! I must concentrate.

When I arrived home, Bert became an absolute pain. Lying on my bed with blankets that had never been used, I started with some violent shakes. I felt hot, very hot, then cold, very cold, with a dreadful headache across my forehead and eyes. I just wanted to be left alone shivering, with the odd hallucination for company.

"You must eat something, lad," said Bert with great authority.

"No thanks, Bert, I just can't", I said, in a shaking voice.

"You must, lad. Everyone's got to eat!"

"No! No, Bert, I'm okay."

"Rubbish, Cy! What about something simple? A bit of egg and bacon, a bit of toast?" Oh no, I was getting nauseated by the minute. "They always make you eat something in 'ospital, lad! Standard practice."

"I'm not in bloody hospital", I said, feeling very cantankerous.

Yet Bert was not to be denied, booming out with, "You've got to eat to provide strength to get over what you've got. It makes sense, lad!". The situation was getting quite unbearable and stressful. Bert being Bert, a self-appointed expert, naturally knew it all. "Go on, I can soon rustle you up something." A real pleading tone was creeping into his voice. He had to succeed and show that he was right. That was Bert.

Just then, Alfie naively pushed into the bedroom, "Hungry yet, Cy?", he said in a worried, mild tone.

Bert immediately exclaimed forcefully, "What the 'ell do you think I've been in here all this time for, you daft whatsit? I've been trying to persuade 'im to eat, so don't you start. I'll get 'im to eat something soon, don't you fret".

"I think you should eat, Cy", whined Alfie!

I whimpered, "Just a jug of water, Bert, please. That's all I want".

"There," said Bert, "What did I tell you? That's a start". This was living proof to Bert that he was succeeding. "Get 'im some water. Go on, 'urry up."

At a distance, faint at first, near the far wall, Emily and Anne's mum, Pen gradually came into the room. Thank God! They'll get me sorted instead of these useless, oafish idiots of men, including that swine of a doctor. I knew my thoughts were wobbly and that I appeared to be dropping into somewhere I had never been before.

Then, in the distance I saw some Toby jugs which had been standing on the shelf lined up behind each other, gradually come closer and closer, in a very threatening manner. Each self-satisfied, grinning face came close up before peeling off as they almost hit my face, with their faces getting bigger than mine. I knew they wished to do me serious harm. They were rapidly multiplying. God, how many of them were there now? It must be an army. I'll show them! I struck out at them repeatedly but didn't even get close to touching them. So I started shouting and really had a go at them. I used all the evil vocabulary I could think of to try and make them go away or upset them, but to no avail.

I felt the heat from a big fire and wondered why they had such a fire. God, it was so hot and seemed to be going on forever. It must have been unbearable to them as it was to me but still they came on and on, one after another. Why attack me? Then gradually their faces started to melt. The melting flesh, a sickening sight. The smell was so bad that I started vomiting as their waxy flesh ran earthwards, their faces contorting, then collapsing. The fire went out and it was freezing cold on my head.

Gradually I realised I was half sat up in bed and a strange lady was holding my head with a cold cloth. She was telling me that it was alright now! What was? Alfie was holding a bowl that I had been sick in. I was wet through with perspiration, including my head. The fire was being put out by cold cloths, applied by this nice lady. She brought reality back by reminding me that she was called Christine, a flat occupant upstairs and that I had repaired her toaster. The lads had been completely out of their depth and had called Christine to come and help see to me.

"Where's Emily and Pen? They were here earlier?", I said. Christine looked bewildered and slowly shook her head, "No, Cy, that was a dream, I think". She also told me that I had been delirious and that she had difficulty in keeping me stable due to me waving my arms around uncontrollably.

Alfie then said very seriously, "You were shouting as well, and not like a gentleman. Terrible it was. Not like you!". Christine gave a sharp look at Alfie, then smiled back at me again. I interpreted her expression as annoyance with Alfie. 'Useless oaf', I thought. Yes, oafish men, including that swine of a doctor! I definitely think that women are the very best!

Looking puzzled as to what he had done or said that was wrong, Alfie got up from the chair and took the bowl away. I had somewhat calmed down now and although I was still very feverish I started to apologise.

"No, Cy, don't try! That was the malaria talking, not you." She was actually smiling, "Quite educational really. I learnt a few new words which could well be used in the right situation". I thought, 'what a great character, just like all women'.

Bert shuffled quietly into the bedroom and asked me how I was. I suspect the events had frightened him. He seemed quite subdued and completely out of his depth. He said that he had been changing the cold towels for Christine and that he was going to make some tea.

Shivering with cold I wanted blankets but the next minute was throwing them off, feeling like a furnace once again. I kept slipping away for short spells and then I drifted off to sleep. It must have been then that Christine left to go back upstairs to her flat.

Later, I went falling into another nightmare. It was then that the lions came! But not at first. I was very close to Nairobi, strolling towards the built-up area in very sparse vegetation. I was amongst tall, thin, leafless trees when I heard the lions roar in the distance. I was off like a shot running and could hear them quite a long way away. They roared again, gradually getting closer. If only I could make the township. I was running for my life now, getting hotter and sweatier by the minute. I was hardly able to breathe, gasping as I desperately tried to keep ahead of them.

They were much closer now. No, I won't give up. Not until they take me. They were much closer now, almost on to me. I could hear their pads striking the earth as I reached the first building. I squeezed through a small gap in the wall and into an open-air alleyway with high brick walls. It was straight and narrow and stretched as far as the eye could see. I've lost the lions, thank God! But I still kept running, knowing I couldn't last much longer. Why was I running? I had to, I just had to.

Then, up in the sky, I saw a plane. It was on fire and was going around and around, dropping slowly down towards the alley. Which way to run? I could hear the roaring of the lions echoing along the walls of the alley! Again, which way to run? Not back towards the lions! Which way, for God's sake! This way, no, the other way. I was oscillating first one way, then the other.

I looked up, petrified. The plane was all thick, black smoke now, still going around and around like a thick solid wheel, dropping very slowly towards me! It was getting bigger and blacker. Nowhere to run now, it wasn't a plane any longer. It hated me and was coming down to devour me.

"No! No! No!" I shouted as my head went first one way and then the other. "No! No! No!" Then someone was with me shouting, "No! No! No!". Thank God! Help at last! But no, they will be eaten also. I screamed, "Get them out, get them out! No! No! No!". My head was desperately going from side to side. I was on fire. It was so hot.

Then slowly, a mist came down. It was a thick mist and slowly and faintly through the mist, a lady's face took shape. The voice, faint at first, was shouting, "No! No! No!", for me. That really helped me! She became clearer, yet still fuzzy. A fair-haired lady was reaching towards me with her arms bent. I could feel her hot palms holding my cheeks. She stopped shouting as I focused on her face. Everything went quiet. I was still boiling hot but the noise had gone! Lifted from me. Even the smoke residue had gone.

This lady, a stranger, was staring into my eyes. I was utterly bewildered. Who is she? Blue eyes I could make out, wet eyes. I stared back at her trying to comprehend, trying to fix my eyes on her through the mist. Her cheeks were tear-stained and straining to concentrate I saw that tears were bubbling over from her eyes and running down a ridge on either side of her nose. All of her face was wet. Poor darling, who was she, and why was she so upset? Her head went away suddenly and I felt it on my chest.

I was drifting into reality. I heard and felt her sobbing as I tried to speak to her. Then a lovely tear-stained smile appeared. Her face was much clearer now. She had fair hair. I felt her arms lightly around my neck and a kiss on the cheek, then she faded away from me. I looked past her and saw Christine. Thank God it's Christine. I know her. Then I saw the fair-haired lady drift through the door. I didn't want her to go. I was so upset that she had gone.

"Hello, Cy." It was Christine. "You are over it now, I'm sure! You're back now! And you're safe!" So that was it. That's what it has been all about! I'm back! Thank God! I'm back! I was terribly shaky and felt like a wreck. I reached slowly up to explore my head. It was wet and my hair was matted. The sweat was drying on my face and tightening my skin yet the whole of my body felt as though it was soaking in wet sheets. What a mess! Horrible thought! Surely I had not wet the bed? No, it must be sweat. I hope so, especially with Christine present. Everything was moving too fast for me. I was so desperately tired but wanted to stay awake. I was too frightened at the thought of going to sleep.

After some time, how long I do not know, I had a cup of tea. Christine was still with me and things were stabilising now. I said to Christine, "I saw a lovely fair-haired lady crying. It upset me very much. I suppose it must have been another dream, like Emily and Pen, yet she was so real!".

"She was not a dream," said Christine. "That was Mary, my friend who is visiting me." Christine was speaking very slowly and deliberately now, which I appreciated. Then looking at me, she paused, and as if making a decision said, "Enough for today, Cy. Bert has rustled up some soup. I'll stay here and help you to eat it if needed. You will be okay once you have eaten". Christine stayed for quite some time, then before leaving said, "I will tell you all about Mary tomorrow when you will be much stronger. I've put clean sheets on the other single bed and when you feel strong enough Bert and Alfie will help you to move into it".

The next time Christine called I was out of bed and sitting in a chair. She came and sat opposite me and told me that she was staying with me for the day because Bert and Alfie had gone back to work at Jinja. "You look much better now that you are taking in food."

"Bert and Alfie don't know much about what happened to me. They said that you will tell me all I want to know." She looked so relaxed in her chair looking at me. I knew I had a lot to thank her for. She had always seemed to be there whenever I had surfaced. I'm glad that I had repaired her toaster!

Smiling she said, "You really want to know about Mary, don't you?".

"What made you think that, Christine?", almost laughing she replied.

"Don't go twinkling your eyes at me, you devil. I'm a married woman. You must be getting better! Save it for Mary, she will be coming to see you later. She is staying with me for a couple of days whilst my husband Jim is away at Soroti." Christine continued, "I invited Mary to stay with me to keep me company and to try and cheer her up a bit. She has been very morose and disinterested in anything going on around her since her husband died about 18 months ago. She was at rock bottom and still had very little interest when she arrived".

"I'm so sorry, Christine", (and I really meant it).

"Yes, she took the death of her husband very badly." Then, with eyes beginning to fill up, and fixing them on mine, she said slowly, "Her husband died in her arms of cerebral malaria".

The last few words shook me. That's very close to home! Christine seemed relieved after she had said that. I knew she was watching my face to see what the reaction was.

She continued, "When Alfie came to get me for the second time Mary had just arrived and was settling in. Alfie was quite distressed and didn't know what to do. He said, 'Cy's in a terrible state with his malaria, can you help us again, Christine?'. He then turned and ran down the stone staircase!

"Mary heard all of this and rushed to me to ask who has malaria. She looked concerned and was all tight and rigid. I told her it was you and that it was bad and she said, 'Come on then, let's go!'. I told her that she mustn't come but she was adamant. With that, she ran past me shouting, 'Come on, I know what to do, Christine. I'll make sure he'll be okay. I'll look after him, leave it to me!', as we both ran down the staircase. She had never even met you before!

"Mary looked shocked when she saw you and momentarily hesitated, but she waded in like a person possessed. She kept desperately shouting at you so close to your face, 'No! No! No!' all the time, with your head in her hands. I was frightened. Both Bert and Alfie quickly disappeared into the lounge. Tears streamed down her face and she was moving your head from side to side. I was seriously thinking of intervening because I was becoming terribly concerned about you. Then I saw your eyes flicker open and when they stayed open I was so relieved.

"Mary was still holding your head, stationary now, staring into your face. Then, she started to sob with her head on your chest. You mumbled something and Mary moved her head very close to your face and gazed at you for some time. When you spoke again she kissed you on the cheek. She stayed a little while watching your face but I think she was emotionally exhausted. She got up from the bed and went back upstairs to my flat.

"She told me later that she cried her heart out until there seemed to be nothing left. It was when Mary left you that I took over. Since your recovery, I have seen a big difference in Mary as well as you, Cy. She is almost back to her old self again."

Slowly as if picking her words, she said, "I think Mary must have a personal hate against malaria. The fact that in her eyes, she was so successful with your recovery, and therefore, victorious, so to speak, over the killer of her husband. I think it became a factor in her recovery. Another factor was when she broke down completely and cried on the bed in my flat, releasing her bottled up grief".

I felt Christine still had something else to say, so I kept quiet. After a long pause, Christine continued with a faraway look in her eyes, "It must have been dreadful for her and so very emotional, reliving such a thing all over again".

With a sudden change of attitude Christine said, "It's time for sustenance! You will be pleased to know that Mary is coming to join us for a bite to eat so I'll get you a G&T first, then busy myself in the kitchen". Good old Christine. G&T. She has definitely got her priorities right! Jim is a fortunate man. When Mary comes I'll thank them both profusely for all they have done for me and when fully recovered, we will all go out and celebrate.

Whilst Christine was in the kitchen I had time to think. Sipping my G&T I lay back in the chair with my thoughts. There was a lot to think about. The great support from Christine, the heights and depths of emotion borne by Mary. Yet nice to think of the healing it had given Mary. Perhaps it was worth my suffering after all. Yes, I do believe it was.

The thought of seeing Mary again quickened my pulse. The really bad thing was that swine of a doctor, Dr Bob. Not even a G&T! Disgusting! Emily will be furious with him!

CHAPTER 18

I found myself checking my appearance before Mary arrived. I do endeavour to be reasonably well-groomed, except on occasions where I've got my head stuck under the bonnet of the car or engaged in other male-dominated, grubby pursuits. Yet, I wished to make as much of an impression as possible on Mary! Why was I making such an effort? To compensate for the last time she had seen me? It could be! I wonder if she is as curious as I am? I doubt it. She had only seen me at rock bottom and it was not a pretty sight to be impressed by.

My memory of Mary was a muzzy face, wet and tear-stained but with a lovely smile. Was that the reason? The lovely smile and the sadness I wished to cure? Maybe that was it because I hadn't a clue as to any of her other characteristics. Height, figure, normal voice and personality. I did not know her!!

On hearing female voices in the kitchen I felt a tinge of apprehension. Mary must have arrived. A little while later, Christine came into the lounge.

"Mary is here" As she spoke Mary appeared in the doorway. She was slightly built with fair hair. She paused at the door, hesitating with shyness and a lack of confidence. I quickly crossed the room to her and then stopped. Both of us were smiling as I did so. To hell with formality! I just opened my arms and hugged her. I felt the hug reciprocated and we both just stayed that way, gaining some sort of mutual strength from each other.

When we drew apart we held each other lightly, searching into each other's face. It brought back the memory of the tears but there weren't any this time. Just a lovely, somewhat delicate face which I didn't want to lose. We both knew then!! Our heads moved forwards and we kissed each other full on the lips and stayed like that for some time. It wasn't a passionate, fearsome kiss, no. It was just a mutual, relaxing, fulfilling togetherness, as though it had been ordained. There were no tears this time. We both had full eyes, but they were not overflowing.

I took her arm and led her to the chair, where she sat down opposite me. Christine said, "Well, what an introduction. Not a word spoken!! Cy, this is Mary. Mary, this is Cy!". We all laughed. A few funny remarks ensued and then Christine excused herself to attend to the kitchen.

I poured Mary a drink and one for myself. Christine was imbibing in the kitchen — a cook's privilege! Mary said, "I really need this, Cy," as she sipped her drink, "I've been so nervous about meeting you again".

"So have I, Mary." We both laughed and agreed on what a daft pair we were. She told me that she worked as a stenographer in a government department. She knew what I did to a certain extent. Obviously, Christine had told her. Once we got started we never seemed to stop talking. Then, Mary got up out of her chair. I, of course, followed suit. She moved around to where the settee was and sat down, patting the cushion next to her, inviting me to join her, which I did. This was much better, much closer. We sat with our heads relaxed on the back of the settee. A little hand crept over, found mine and we sat there holding hands and talking.

Christine came in and feigning surprise, "Oh! I see you've moved! You both look so comfortable sitting there. I'm sorry to have to disturb you, but lunch is ready!".

Manweri (who normally would have cooked the lunch) was still away at his 'Shamba' upcountry and wouldn't be back until the date I was scheduled to return.

During lunch, Christine said, "Emily should be back home tomorrow so you will have a real, live nursing sister to keep an eye on you, Cy!".

Humorously I said, "Knowing Emily she will, of course, have to put everything back into its place before she visits". Everyone in the local community knew how meticulous Emily was.

During lunch, mutual eye meetings were almost continuous. I thought she was growing more beautiful by the minute. Hurry up, Cy!! Get your strength back to normal, this girl needs taking out. She has to be wined and dined and she mustn't be allowed to slip back into misery again.

Mary had to leave before it got dark, to return to her flat at Nakasero. After an affectionate farewell, Mary went home leaving me in a very thoughtful state of mind. Christine brought me out of my thoughts with a "Well, that was one hell of an introduction. You've both really hit it off, haven't you?".

"You could say that, Christine. Mary has a lovely personality and is so attractive. She certainly has given me the incentive to get back into circulation once again."

"It has been a hectic few days. You gave me a terrible fright and now it is all over I feel like a wet rag."

Looking at Christine sitting opposite, I realised that indeed she did look tired and it was all my fault. But she had lovely hazel eyes, which were still lively and full of expression, something that Jim must appreciate. Strange this life of ours. I've always found brown eyes most attractive in a woman. They have a real depth and I am so drawn to them. Yet Anne did not have brown eyes and neither does Mary.

I had become very fond of Christine. She was so reliable and had an engaging personality. She knew how I appreciated her attributes and the unstinting help she had given me during and after my malaria, and this had helped to make us good friends.

Bert and Alfie arrived home to join us. After a short interval, Christine got up out of the chair to leave me in their care. Jim would also be home tomorrow and she needed to prepare. She came over to me and said, "Could I have a hug now please before I go?". Of all the people she surely needed and deserved a hug. As she withdrew from her very close hug, she kissed me on the cheek, "I feel better for that, Cy", she said.

Cheekily I said, "Oh yes, Christine so do I."

"You are a rogue and greedy with it! I must warn Mary." And with a wink she went up the stone staircase to her flat. I wonder if… No, Cy!! Of course not, definitely not!!

Bert and Alfie were their normal selves now that I was back on my feet again. Bert told me they would be returning to their hotel in Jinja tomorrow. He said, "All in all staying here has been different, to say the least, but the journey to and from Jinja every day is getting to be a bit tiring". I thought he must be joking as it's only 50 miles!! Of course, they were both a lot older and 'settled'. Personally, I think they wanted out. It probably was bliss before I returned with my problem, which certainly upset their cosy routine and now they were worried in case some other catastrophe appeared on the scene. They should really be at 'ome in the UK with their slippers to hand.

The next evening Emily called in to see me! After a hug and pleasantries, she said, "You've lost weight! We will have to get that back on! So, you've had malaria?!". How did she know? No doubt I'll soon find out.

"Yes. Emily. I don't know why, I'm sure I've always taken my pills!"

"Mmm!! I've been thinking about that. Which day of the week do you take it?"

"Always after breakfast on a Friday."

"Well, well. That fits then doesn't it?" I must have looked bewildered. "It was mid-morning Friday when you were so badly ill with food poisoning at Nakuru. That would result in the non-absorption of the pill. That's why you contracted malaria, Cy!" So that was it, that damned food poisoning. I never thought of a connection!

"Bob has got it now!", Emily continued.

"Bob who?"

"Bob Milne, Dr Bob Milne. You know him well enough!" She was looking at me ever so quizzically, "Bob has got malaria!".

Well, well, what a hypocrite! Preaching to me and casting me into the dungeon because I had contracted it. Telling me how Emily will be so cross with me for having it. My, my! I can hardly believe it. What possible excuse can he have for getting it? Ho ho ho! I can't wait for him to get better. Seriously I said, "How is he, Emily?".

"Well, I phoned the hospital as soon as I arrived home to let them know I was back in residence and his wife Laura answered. It seems he is not too bad at all. Not like you, it seems it was a close shave with you, Cy, according to Christine and Mary!" Aha! Mystery solved — that's how she knew!

"You've met Mary then, Emily?"

"Oh yes, I've known Mary for some time. I knew her husband also. I joined Christine and Mary having coffee in the Athenian. They called me over to their table and told me what a grim time was had with your malaria. Mary seems to have taken a real shine to you!"

"Oh yes, Emily? What have they been saying?"

"Nothing, Cy. Nothing was said but it was obvious to me, being another woman. You wouldn't have picked up the signs being a thick-headed male. No offence, all males are the same. No intuition! Anyway, it was confirmed to me by Christine when we got back here to the flats."

There was a bit of a lull in the conversation. Then, Emily fixed me with one of her very old-fashioned, funny looks. I wondered what was coming next. Not for long!

"She is an exceptionally nice girl is Mary. So don't you go spoiling it all!"

Expressing false hurt I said, "What the devil do you mean by that, Emily?"

"You know full well what I mean, you dog! You've been eyeing me up for months, wondering how to tackle the fortress. It has been giving me endless amusement. I will never forget the look in your eyes when I emerged as a St. Trinian's girl when we did that fancy dress party. I expected that I would have had to repel borders then, but you did exceptionally well to contain yourself."

"I was frightened of you, that's why". We were both laughing now. "I didn't receive one microscopic part of encouragement from you, Emily."

"That's because I don't give you any. I expect you to contain yourself and to keep your hands to yourself! If I gave you this so-called microscopic part of encouragement I know you would take immediate advantage of it." I didn't realise that she knew me that well! Shrewd little sod, our Emily!! Yet such a good friend to have around.

Yes, I had made the correct evaluation of her on the train viz. "She had her principles and would abide by them. She would make a loyal friend — platonically, of course!!". Naturally, being a complete optimist I had always hoped that I had been wrong in my assessment of her and that she might, one day, stray off the path slightly and pick a few daisies. Not a hope!!

I don't suppose I was different from any other rampant Aries male in their prime!!

No comment, please!

CHAPTER 19

It was ten days later that I saw Bob's colleague, Dr Bill Broady, who pronounced me fit. To celebrate the return to normality and to register a gesture of thanks for all the help that I had been given, I organised a meal at The City Bar for Christine, Jim, Mary and I.

We had a very good evening, which was enhanced by the meeting and company of flat neighbours, Les and June (husband and wife), who joined us after dinner for drinks. I was heeding Emily's directive and behaving myself with Mary, treading softly-softly. I thought a lot of her and I knew it was reciprocated. I also realised that she still had lots of hurt over her husband's death, and therefore, it would have been very unkind and unfeeling of me to quicken the pace of our relationship. It was very rewarding just being with her.

One day Emily suggested that I should visit the hospital for a check-up. I told her that I didn't think it was necessary, but she was, and can be, very persuasive as you can probably guess. So I duly presented myself at the hospital at the allotted time.

Guess who the duty doctor was! Yes, it was Bob! I walked into his surgery and there he was sitting behind his desk, hands up in the air feigning token surrender! Then, prominently displayed on the desk, I saw a bottle of gin with two glasses already primed with G&Ts, plus a card which read, 'Profound apologies, Cy. I'd had a terribly bad day'.

I gave him some of my friendly expletives (just to show that he hadn't got away with it completely) and told him that Emily, far from being cross with me had deducted many brownie points from his card. Never one to bear a grudge we drank our G&Ts and once again became amicable. Bob said, "This was Emily's doing, suggesting you have a 'check-up' to allow me to give you an abject apology. Now you are here I might as well run the rule over you, once again. But you look fit now". The rule was run over me and confirmed his opinion.

Mary and I saw each other at every opportunity, except when I was on emergency call. She said, "I am worried each time you are called out. You go out and you never know what you might find. It could be very dangerous, especially in the storms and in those out of town places".

To save her from the worry and anxiety we agreed not to see each other during the evenings when I was on emergency call, then she wouldn't know what I was up to. Of course, we kept in touch by phone and met sometimes during the day at lunchtime.

One day Mary suggested that we invite Christine, Jim, June and Les for dinner at her flat. She had so enjoyed our time with them at The City Bar and thought it would be nice to have another get together. I agreed that it was a splendid idea. We arranged it for a Saturday evening on a week when I was not on call.

I had made myself presentable and arrived at Mary's flat before the others so that we would have a little time on our own. This served the additional purpose of being on hand to serve drinks on their arrival.

Mary employed a house girl named Julie. She was a good cook and on occasions very flamboyant. She was tubby with a large bottom, an attribute which was a figure of beauty in the Baganda tribe. Especially so through the eyes of the male members. When dressing up the Baganda women would often wrap layers of material around their bottoms, to increase the size. In the 1950s, Tootal Fabrics were the most popular who manufactured brilliant colours. I should think the Baganda women must have influenced Tootal's profit margin. Julie took advantage of this wealth of cheap fabric and as a result, always looked large and colourful. She smiled easily, laughed a lot when I teased her and was devoted to Mary.

My Swahili had become so natural to me it was just like speaking

English. New horizons were opening up in respect that I could laugh and joke on the same wavelength, understand their outlook, and recognise their simple humour. So much so that I was always ready to have fun with Ugandans and yet avail myself to sort out their problems. Because of this bonding and my British sense of justice, I was held in great respect.

I often teased Julie, especially when she had a new or different colour wrap around. Lifting my arms and eyes to heaven I would say "Maradadi sana kabisa", which means 'the most beautiful as it is possible to be'. Her big eyes got bigger and she would slap her thighs laughing.

"Bwana mjinga sana" she would say, (Bwana very funny).

I once teased her about her many boyfriends. She thought it hugely funny when I said, "Mingi dawa Julie", (lots of medicine), because previously I had asked her, "You have all these boyfriends, why no watoto?".

She said, "Dawa we take from the bush". She wouldn't tell me what or from where! Even in the 1950s, it does appear that the Africans in Uganda (and probably elsewhere) were practising a form of birth control, gained from a natural source, i.e. from the trees. Looking around in that era one noticed that the African family was not overburdened with children. There must have been something in use other than abstinence (God forbid). Yes, food for thought isn't it?

I did notice how conscientious Julie was in the kitchen. Anything to be eaten raw (for example, salad, lettuce, tomatoes, fruit etc.), were left in water in the sink with crystals of potassium permanganate, releasing oxygen to kill all germs. It prevented tummy bug infections similar to the serious food poisoning I had at Nakuru. At Nakuru, I was the only one affected, so it was assumed that some swine of a fly had tasted my breakfast before going back to his home in the dung heap.

Returning from Julie and my digression. The others arrived and we were all soon talking. Mary was loving it and I was so happy for her. Eventually, we were called to the table by Julie who looked splendid in her multicoloured pinny. Halfway through the meal, the phone rang. Julie answering it in the lounge. She came into the dining room and said, "It's for you, Bwana!".

Mary and I exchanged glances whilst I excused myself and went to the phone.

"Sir," said the telephone operator, " there is no communication with Nairobi, or Jinja, or Mombasa, sir".

"Tell the emergency engineer, not me!!"

"I can't find him, sir. There is no reply from his phone." I asked the operator if a forwarding number was given to him to ring. "No, sir".

Being the Maintenance Control Officer, it was my responsibility. "Okay," I said, "Thank you, I will deal with it". Mary overheard my side of the conversation and her eyes were widening by the second.

"What's wrong, Cy? It's not your night on. It's not fair! Do you have to go?"

"The duty engineer can't be raised so it becomes my responsibility, Mary."

I gave my apologies to Mary's guests and explained the problem. Mary came with me to the door and holding on to my arm, said, "Phone me and tell me what's happening, Cy. When you know the circumstances". Her face a mixture of disappointment and concern.

I arrived at the Communication Centre and hoped the fault was at Jinja, perhaps with the radio link. But on researching the Carrier Room I diagnosed the fault to be 15 miles along the Jinja road. Every circuit was down, constituting a major emergency. Looking at the detailed map the route ran close to the road in the Mabira forest.

I rang everyone for assistance, but it was Saturday night. Still, each houseboy promised to tell his Bwana on his return, to go to mile 15 on the Jinja road. I impressed on each houseboy how important it was and I had to be content with that! I looked over towards Jinja and could see lightning in the distance and thought of the pleasant evening I was going to lose.

I rang Mary with the bad news. She was upset, "Come back here when the fault is cleared, no matter what time it is, even if our guests have gone home. Promise me?". I promised and told her not to worry. Mary, dear Mary. She must feel so insecure. If she knew how I felt she wouldn't worry. To me, call outs were just a damn nuisance and part of my job. It was a pity and unfortunate that this one had spoilt our lovely evening and it seemed worse because I was not officially on call.

I went into the yard and checked the 'bus' so nicknamed, a big lorry with all the attachments. Floodlights, a winch, ladders, cables, bronze and copper wire coils, just about everything, except the kitchen stove. I drove out of the yard, closed the gates behind me, went down to the main road and turned out on to the Jinja road, into the darkness. There didn't appear to be any 'sky fireworks' ahead as I trundled along with the noisy, heavy engine. The storm must have gone. I was dressed in nice, clean, lightweight cream slacks and shirt. I've forgotten which colour but being a mere male, I wouldn't remember, would I? I think I've done well to remember which slacks I had on! Anyway, it wasn't the ideal attire for the job I now envisaged. There was no way could I go back to Kololo to change.

The pole route affected was the main trunk route of communication between Uganda and Kenya. Instead of the usual single pole, the timber poles (which were heavy-duty and very tall), were doubled one yard apart and connected with steel struts for stability. They carried heavy-duty wire conductors. Having dual poles also meant that the longer arms across the two poles could be fitted to provide many more circuits.

Each pair of conductors carried twelve circuits. I.e. twelve speaking channels and teleprinter circuits, including quite vital teleprinter circuits from the international airport at Entebbe. The twelve circuits on each pair of wires operated on different frequencies and were therefore completely separate from each other. They were filtered and sorted into separate speech channels, known as junctions, by technical equipment in the Carrier Room, inside the Communications Building. Because of the vast distances involved, the conductors couldn't run parallel with each other. Instead, they had to be transposed (which is quite a complicated procedure) to prevent an electrical field development which could cause cross-talk. This had to be considered when re-erecting the conductors. This is as short and as sweet as I can make the technical stuff!!

Eventually, I saw it. The pole route was on the right-hand side of the road. Heavy wires hung down due to a tall gum tree that had fallen and was lying across the pole route. The normally narrow road ditch (which was between the road and the pole route), was now a raging torrent and far too dangerous to contemplate crossing. It was also very dark on the edge of the forest with everything dripping after the storm.

The trouble with gum trees is that they are so tall but light and their shallow roots can cause them to become unstable in violent weather. I switched the floodlight on to the scene. It was not a pretty sight. I took one of the large extension ladders down, stretched it out and let it fall on comparatively firm ground on the other side of the torrent, making a bridge.

I went across on all fours to get to grips with the problem, thinking that anything watching me from inside the forest will be utterly confused as to what was walking on all four legs towards them. It was a mess but not unsurmountable. I could do with some help! And ropes, also a panga (machete) from the truck.

I went back to the truck, found a length of chain and set about trying to attach it around the tree. But there were myriads of branches and soft growth to be hacked away first with the panga. I managed to attach a rope to the chain but would need assistance to operate and control the winch. Great care would be needed to avoid further damage.

There was still a massive number of branches, growth and other debris to hack away and remove before contemplating the removal of the tree. It was also difficult to see and feel the tree growth and I was a little wary as to what I was putting my hand on in the semi-darkness. I also felt that I was being watched by many pairs of eyes behind me in the forest.

Nearing midnight I heard a car stop and then another from the direction of Jinja. Someone shouted, "Hello!!". I answered back and extracted myself from the debris. It was Bari, a well-built Asian man who was most obliging, friendly and helpful. Yes, it would be Bari who would stop. He had seen the truck of course. He could now see the problem and went back to the cars on the road, where Asian voices and slamming doors could be heard. Bari was nicely dressed and was returning home with his family and friends from Jinja. "My cousin from the other car will drive my family home", said Bari. It wasn't his concern, but he made it his concern to be involved. He could quite easily have driven on, especially as he was in his best bib and tucker, like me.

Within a space of a few minutes, two more cars arrived from Kampala with assistance from the administration. One car even contained a couple of extra volunteers! They had all been out for the evening and received the message upon returning home. Unlike Bari and I, they were able to change. It was after midnight and I hadn't realised that it was so late. Mary will be worrying!

We organised a program of work and then Lumpus arrived in his car. He had been out for the evening also. We nicknamed him Lumpus but it would be inappropriate here to say why. Lumpus was tall, brilliantly technical and married to Bessie who was a petite and endearing person. Everybody just loved Bessie! Lumpus had a slight disadvantage. He only had one eye after losing the other one during his youth. He made light of this affliction and often turned it to his advantage when the occasion presented itself.

He, like the others, was full of extra confidence after an evening out imbibing. He watched as two of the gang crossed the ladder bridge on all fours, then exclaimed with great bravado, "What's the matter with you monkeys, why don't you walk across?". With that remark, Lumpus confidently strode onto the ladder and promptly fell in. He grabbed a thick root from the bank and hung on as the water tried its utmost to dislodge him and sweep him downstream.

Brian, another colleague, missed his footing trying to clutch at Lumpus but only managed to be submerged up to his waist. He was now holding on to Lumpus and we were all holding on to both of them and to each other. We were slipping and sliding, trying desperately to keep on our feet in thick, runny mud and not always succeeding! The scene could have easily been taken from a silent comedy film.

After much bad language we extracted the two unfortunates. All of us were absolutely covered in mud. Then, it started! "You blinked your wrong eye, Lumpus", and "You must have been looking on your blind side, Lumpus". There was great esprit de corps amongst us. Of course, being in Uganda the water wasn't cold. But as Lumpus remarked, "I feel distinctly uncomfortable around my nether regions, I hope I haven't taken any baby frogs on board!!".

It took us until 3:30 am to re-terminate, regulate the heavy conductors and restore the route. After putting the bus to bed I was in two minds. Mary had said to come back no matter what time it is, but 4 am? Still! She had made me promise! The guests will have gone home — that is a sure bet. She will be fast asleep. Do I disturb her? Surely not at this ungodly hour and the state I am in. Yet, I had promised!

I pulled up outside Mary's flat as quiet as I could be. Everywhere was in darkness. Standing on the doorstep I was undecided whether to ring the bell when suddenly the light came on, the door opened and a tousled-haired Mary flung her arms around my neck. I was on the lower step so she was able to do so.

She said, "Being so late I thought you had decided to go home. Then I thought something had happened to you so I haven't really slept. But I heard you pull up". She was in a very thin dressing gown which activated my senses. I don't suppose there were any thick ones in Uganda. As I moved through the doorway into the light, Mary moved back and looked wide-eyed and shocked. A bemused smile followed.

"What a mess! Just look at yourself! Your lovely slacks and shirt and even your shoes. And your face!" Then, laughing with both hands to her cheeks she surveyed me up and down. "Where the hell have you been?"

"Playing in the Mabira forest!"

With an incredulous look on her face, "Well, it is now time to play in the shower". She moved to me and put her arms loosely around my neck. "I can't wait to hear what you have been up to. You can tell me all about it later. At least your slacks and shirt are dry. I can brush off any loose mud whilst you are in the shower. I'm afraid I don't stock any gentleman's attire in my flat." Moving her head until we were cheek to cheek she whispered, "I'll make you a nice cup of coffee with a touch of brandy. That will do you good after your shower".

I felt much better once I was all nice and clean and sipping coffee. Surveying my clothes I thought Mary had done well. They looked smoother and now had an army camouflage look about them.

Finishing my coffee coincided with Mary coming out from the bathroom. She came across the room to me looking quite serious and slowly, bending down to me in the chair, placed both her hands on the chair arms until we were touching noses. We gently rubbed noses and then kissed. We pulled away slightly, then almost nose to nose and looking deep into each other's eyes, she said, "Come to bed, pet. You are not going home".

This was totally unexpected. I had sensed a closer feeling between us recently and especially so this evening. I had resisted the overwhelming desire to move more into a physical phase, out of respect for Mary, as previously mentioned. But this evening I could feel a different, more urgent sense when we kissed. A faint tremor when we embraced and knew that something had to give way soon. I thought that Mary realised it also, yet it was still completely unexpected.

Even though I was tired I could certainly cope!! Today of course, at the age I am now and, in those circumstances, (i.e. at 4 am after playing in the forest all night), well… cope? I think it would be open to debate!

Mary had a typical girl's bedroom. It was pinkish with a few cuddly toys. She had a three-quarter size bed which was bigger than the standard single supplied by the administration. How had she wangled that?

It was such a heavenly night, or should I say morning. I woke up first, late of course! The pigeons once again!! There always seemed to be pigeons cooing when I woke up. Looking sideways I gazed on Mary's face deep in slumberland. She was so pretty with no makeup. It was nice to see her like this. Just like a child asleep. It stirred all the tender feelings I had for her, especially as she had given herself to me with so much love during the early hours. The fulfilment had been needed by both of us.

She looked so relaxed and calm, then she stirred and one eye flickered open. Her face lit up and a smile started to develop. "You've been looking at me!"

"That's quite right, I have. I think you are very nice in bed!"

Her smile deepened, "You too". Snuggling up she said, "Let's just stay here all day. I feel so much happier and contented".

"That makes two of us."

We chatted away for some time before Mary said, "I can't let you go home on a Sunday looking like a grubby little boy. I will go and see Manweri who will sort out fresh slacks, a shirt and shorts. Then I will bring them back here. We will have a lovely day together".

There was a knock on the door. Julie had heard us talking and brought in two teas. She wore a hugely happy smile on her face.

"Mjambo Bwana! Mjambo Memsaab! Mzuri Bwana, mzuri sana kwa Memsaab!!" Which translates to: 'Good morning, Bwana! Good morning,

Memsaab! It is good Bwana, and very good for Memsaab!!'. She was so happy with the new arrangement.

CHAPTER 20

Mary and I had now formed a close friendship with Christine, Jim, June and Les. The six of us enjoyed most of our leisure time and activities together.

Jim was a salesman who had to make quite a few trips around Uganda dealing with sales of hydraulic equipment. He was slightly built, thin-faced and grey-eyed with dark hair receding from his forehead. His happy and warm personality was reflected in his ready smile.

Les was a police superintendent and had dark hair (more of it than Jim!). He was quite handsome with dry, witty humour. As well as being a superintendent, he was also the heavyweight boxing champion of Uganda! As you might expect he was large in size with huge, broad shoulders. He was a perfect partner for June who was full of fun. She was medium in height and slender with lovely, long, deep golden hair.

Before being promoted and posted to Kampala, Les worked in an area nearer to the Sudan border where the indigenous population comprised mostly of primitive tribesmen. They were fascinated by June's hair and would come from far and wide to admire her and try to touch and stroke it.

Because of her hair, they called her "Memsaab Simba" (lion). June at that time was new to Uganda, having been delayed in the UK because of family problems. Whereas, Les was already well and truly settled in his police work.

To June it was a somewhat apprehensive time. Straight from living in a town in a civilised community she was thrust into a foreign country in close proximity to fierce, wild-looking tribesmen wearing nothing except for a draped cloth-like blanket, intent on innocently getting closer to admire and stroke her hair. June had us in stitches when recalling that period, exaggerating the circumstances, of course, as June would do.

The six of us got on so well together. All had a form of ready wit, making every occasion a jolly one. And if Jim was away upcountry, Christine certainly contributed her share of the fun.

When Les had to take part in boxing contests the girls generally stayed at June's flat to enjoy lovely, girls evenings. June was a dressmaker and had all the tools of the trade, so you can no doubt imagine what it was like when the men went to the boxing arena. The girls had the run of the very spacious flat, covering the lounge area with patterns, pins, and material mostly from Tootal Fabrics, which was ideal for making simple cotton skirts and dresses etc. To the male, it was a most bewildering and seemingly disorganised scene of activity, but to the ladies, it was a great evening without any male encumbrance.

I generally went early with Les to the boxing ring and Jim came occasionally when he was not employed upcountry. It was often a charity boxing contest held for the benefit of local children. His opponent on these occasions was Idi Amin, the light heavyweight boxing champion of Uganda, who was a sergeant in the King's African Rifles. After the contest Les and I, along with a few other individuals (who were mostly army personnel), were invited into the sergeant's mess for post-fight celebration drinks.

Idi was a superbly fit boxer with a fine physique and was known by most people as Idi Amin. However, he preferred to be called Idi Amin Dada (both a's pronounced as in Dad). He was very pro-European, recognising the help that we were giving to the people of Uganda, especially in the investment and the building of the infrastructure. During our many discussions, it became obvious that he admired the British monarchy, especially Her Majesty the Queen. We had many laughs with Idi who always threatened to beat Les in the ring "next time". I said,

"Keep on eating the army bully beef, Idi. Then one day you will and on that day I hope that I will have my money on you." Yes, they were very good evenings with lots of good health being drunk.

When I returned to the UK and heard that Idi had replaced the head of state (Milton Obote) I was flabbergasted! It was incredible! Idi Amin surely had no experience or educational qualifications to enable him or to even contemplate the running of a country. He was a sergeant in the army. Milton Obote on the other hand was an out-and-out nationalist who had led the Uganda People's Congress and had legislative knowledge which had somewhat prepared him to run the country.

During a previous small party at The City Bar, some of us had teased Milton Obote, saying to him that if we stayed to work in Uganda after the country had gained independence we might physically lose our heads if he became head of state. He laughed with us, enjoying the banter and said, "I would do no such thing. Justice will prevail if I am in power".

It was a friendly evening but I could not bring myself to serve under him no matter what the inducements, even with all his friendly gestures and charm. I just did not trust the man. There would not be any world-renowned British justice in the country and heads could roll (and did) with just one whim or command.

So, although very surprised and shocked that Idi Amin had ousted Milton Obote, I was happy that such a cruel murderer of many souls had now gone. Although Idi Amin would not have the knowledge required to run the country, he was a very likeable, friendly, pro-British character. With good administrative help I was sure he would succeed and bring well overdue justice for the mass of such loveable people. How very, very wrong I was. How and why, oh why did he develop into an even worse tyrant than Milton Obote? Many people must have their own theories as to the cause, including myself, but only Idi Amin Dada really knew!!

CHAPTER 21

It was now accepted by the community that Mary and I were a couple, living together either at Kololo or Nakasero. Manweri, now back in my flat at Kololo and Julie in Mary's flat at Nakasero, promoted their own personalities. Although Manweri approved of the Bwana and Memsaab situation wholeheartedly, he was much quieter than Julie and sometimes it was difficult to know what he was thinking. I had known him for quite a long time and understood his quiet ways. He was a family man!

He returned from his Shamba upcountry, bringing his wife, small baby and little boy back with him knowing that he was settled in a good job. I know he approved of Mary. She was so friendly, quiet and had an understanding nature. By showing much affection to his little boy with her natural love for children, she overcame his son's shyness on meeting a white woman. So much so that the little boy positively beamed at her whenever he saw her. In turn, whenever I mentioned that Mary was coming, I noticed Manweri's eyes light up. Lightly smiling he would say, "Muzuri Bwana!", (It is good Bwana!).

As for Julie, she wore her feelings upfront for all to see. Boisterously excitable and happy whenever I arrived, she was always willing to make me one of her scrumptious fruit salads from all the local fruits possible. I had much fun with Julie teasing her. Julie's noisy laughter would reverberate around the flat. Mary used to joke, "I'll have to keep my eye on you two!".

In my flat, we had two single beds, whereas Mary had her three-quarter sized bed. This was an added attraction, except for when it was unbearably hot and sticky, which unfortunately was the norm. Whenever I was on call we stayed at my place, which would make the disturbance minimal, having single beds in the event of being called out.

Mary, although loathing the thought of me going out at night, now preferred to stay with me at Kololo. I wasn't called out every time I was on call, yet on occasions, it could be more than once in a night.

We saw Emily quite often, mostly at her flat playing Canasta or just for tea and sometimes at my flat next door. Geoff (my friend from the forestry) sometimes joined us to make up a foursome, especially so when we were playing cards. He was a great asset in company and was basically on the same wavelength as I in his attitude towards the fairer sex.

Now that I was with Mary, Geoff of course had a clear field. It was natural that I assisted him with his endeavours, in company and in conversations whenever possible, by putting in a vital word to promote or to increase the interest of the lady he wished to impress.

Mary and I now had some nice friends and enjoyed our leisure time in full. The ladies enjoyed their own get-togethers on occasions when one of the cars needed a de-coke or major attention and the men were engaged as a consequence.

Mary became very concerned when she received a telephone call from John, one of her two brothers who lived at Mbale in Eastern Uganda. John said that he had to return to the UK to face a charge of fraud. Consequently, both John and Clive (her younger brother) would be coming to Kampala en route to Entebbe airport. Clive asked if he could stay with us for a few days at Mary's flat after John had departed for the UK. We both heartily agreed and arranged to have a few days off work to spend with Clive.

I hadn't met her brothers so I thought it a splendid idea for me to get to know them. Mary, in a preview about her brothers, had told me that it was accepted by her family that John was the black sheep, tending to court disaster by sailing too close to the wind as far as the law was concerned. Clive on the other hand was a confirmed bachelor at such an early stage of his life and the complete opposite. He was serious-minded and quiet, with characteristics similar to the proverbial church mouse.

Both John and Clive were employed by a firm of accountants until recently when John was relieved of his duties as soon as his summons dropped onto the office mat. They both arrived mid-afternoon on our last working day and were settled at Mary's flat when we arrived home. Julie had seen to that. She just loved people visiting and made them welcome as only Julie could.

After introductions, I weighed them up. John was plump with a big face and receding dark hair. He looked as though he had been the dominant and the better fed one in the nest. I found him to be somewhat overbearing and utterly sure of himself. I could see how he could be easily involved in fraud. It is naughty to pre-judge but that is how he impressed me. Clive, by contrast, was a little smaller in height and fairer. His softer nature and personality was similar to Mary. Clive was a "we" person, not a first-person. It was always "We can" and rarely "I can".

When John left for the airport en route to the UK, I wished him success with the trial ahead of him. Yet, in my mind was the surety that he was the villain. The vehicle, which John and Clive were driving, intrigued me. It was a four-wheel-drive safari type truck. It was quite powerful, yet it had a distinctive homemade look about it. Whilst questioning Clive about the vehicle on his return from the airport, he said that John had bought it from an enthusiastic motor mechanic who had 'married' the engine and transmission to a chassis, which has an unusual homemade constructed body. It had a curved metal shield shaped like an American covered wagon with a metal door at the rear end, similar to the modern-day hatchback. John had told Clive that it offered more security.

"Security from what, Clive?", I asked.

"Ah, just security! John said it was secure — not me!" I left it at that.

"Have you been anywhere special in it, Clive? Perhaps a Safari?"

"No, not really. We just use it as a run around vehicle. John thought it looked impressive." What a waste of vehicle!!

To me, Clive seemed so formal. Unable to unbend and took everything so literally. Jokes were wasted on him. I gathered he was a man of principle, but he needed motivating. Alas, he was happy the way he was. So be it! Thoughts of a safari were giving birth inside my head alongside the lateral appraisal of Clive.

The next day I talked to Mary about the possibility of the three of us going on safari in the truck. It would be nice to show Clive around this part of the country.

"Where to, Cy?"

"Quite a choice really. There is one place I would love to visit and I must go someday if not now."

"Where's that?"

"Murchinson Falls where the Victoria Nile crashes its way through a narrow gap on its eventual way to Egypt."

"Murchinson Falls!?", exclaimed Mary, her eyes mightily enlarged and her eyebrows almost reaching the top of her head. "Murchinson Falls? It is a very dangerous place to go from all accounts, isn't it? Especially with all those wild animals and primitive natives."

She stared at me, then paused during which a vague, cunning expression in her eyes took over. Her gaze then centred on the floor. A woman's look, that can often trigger a bout of nervousness in the less devious male. Before I had time to analyse her expression she suddenly said, all bright-eyed and somewhat enthusiastically (which surprised me), "Yes darling, if that is where you would like to go. It will be a break for us and it will be okay as far as I am concerned. As long as I am with you".

I thought, 'that was easy'. I did not expect her to agree! Wonderful! No need for me to plead, she's not as nervous as I thought she was. She must feel safe with me — that's what it must be. It gave me a great egotistical booster injection which the male member of the species readily accepts.

She continued, "I don't think Clive will be impressed. He is basically a town man". She had an odd, enthusiastic, yet comical expression on her face which I was trying to fathom. "Let's call him in and ask him."

Clive had been talking to William (a flat neighbour of Mary's) and was just coming through the door.

"Ah! Just the man. We've got an idea." Clive came in and sat down with a normal, yet inquisitive face. Mary was also sat down opposite me but with her face turned towards the window. I could see that she was trying her utmost not to laugh. I noticed Clive's expression change as he looked at Mary with a puzzled, uncomprehending look.

"Fancy going up to have a look around Murchinson Falls, Clive? Just the three of us for a little break from routine?" His head swung around immediately.

Staring at me he said, "Murchinson Falls? Mmm". He then looked down at the carpet and gently bit his lip. I could see Mary was having difficulty controlling herself and I was beginning to get the drift.

"Mmm, well," he said, "I don't think we should be going up there, Cy, what with all that wild game. It could be dangerous! There's just about everything up there. It's very primitive!".

I couldn't believe it. Turning down a chance of a safari in a safari truck to an area teeming with big game. Where was the adventurous spirit? To see life in the wild, the animals in their natural habitat. This is like an Alec scene but without the Mau Mau. I thought I would have had to convince Mary, not Clive!

"Clive, why have a safari truck if you don't use it? It looks like a good vehicle." Then with another persuasive thrust, "There is an armed ranger up there now since it was recently classified as a game park area in 1952". He was looking distinctly nervous and apprehensive about the whole concept, just like Alec had been when I had suggested the Thika trip from Nairobi.

Suddenly, Mary got up from her chair and left the room in a hurry. Her face was turned away from us presumably to hide an embarrassing breakdown into laughter. Clive stared at her. His head turned and his eyes followed her, wondering what was the matter with his sister.

As soon as she had left the room I said with a lowered voice, "It will be good for Mary to have a different type of break. She is so looking forward to it, going up there".

"Really?"

"Yes, Clive, she is."

"Well, well, well. I can hardly believe it. I wouldn't have thought it would appeal to her. She's so scared of wild animals and primitive areas. She has always been one for a quiet life like me. She has changed. I can hardly believe it."

"Look at it this way, Clive. As I said before she needs a holiday and she is so looking forward to it. Between you and me she is so delighted that you are here, especially as she has not seen you for such a long time." His face was a picture of doubt and concern. I said, "I don't want to disappoint her after all that she has been through". God forgive me!

"I can't believe she has changed so much!"

Just then, Mary re-joined us looking a little more stable and a trifle smug.

"Cy says you are looking forward to this trip to Murchinson Falls, Mary."

After a slight pause and a quick glance at me she said, "Yes, I am". Clive looked at his sister with a puzzled expression.

"I wouldn't have thought it was our scene. Wild animals, no town facilities, plus all the danger. If you are really looking forward to it so much then I'll come along, but I don't like the sound of it!"

"Oh great, Clive," I said, cutting in before Mary had a chance to speak. "Brilliant! We've all got something to look forward to." Mary was staring at me like a little girl watching the magician pull a rabbit from a hat.

Eventually, Clive left the room and Mary quickly left her chair, came very close and looking at me with utter disbelief whispered, "How the hell did you persuade Clive?". She was actually glaring at me! "I never would have thought in my wildest dreams that Clive would agree to come. I only agreed to come knowing full well that Clive would veto it. I am scared to death of going up there! What did you say to him for goodness sake?"

"Just a man-to-man talk, darling."

"Is that all!? There must have been something magical or very fishy in that conversation. I still can't believe it!"

In bed that night I told her that there was nothing to worry about and nothing to be frightened of. Excitement yes, but that's living. "I'll be there and I promise I won't leave you for a moment."

"You can bet your sweet life on that, Cy. You'll feel as though we are joined at the hip."

The next day I looked over the vehicle with Clive and prepped it ready to go the following day. Clive suggested I drive. "John always drove it, Cy. I'm not keen". It suited me fine, Clive was so slow in making decisions.

We were set to go quite early but Clive, who loved his bed, did not arise. Julie took him a cup of tea but Clive just told her to leave it on the floor by his bed. He wasn't quite ready to drink it. He succumbed to an extra dose of shuteye and awoke with Mary banging on his door.

A few minutes later there were shouts and painful sounds coming from his bedroom. Julie, Mary and I arrived at his door at the same time. He stood there in pyjamas (I couldn't believe it in Uganda — I didn't wear anything in bed and I still don't!). There was a most horrified look on his face. One hand was holding his cup, the other hand was rubbing his lips.

"I hope I haven't been poisoned!", he exclaimed between facial contortions. Julie sucked in a large breath. Then, thrusting his cup at arm's length, "Just look!". Julie looked frightened because she had brought the 'poisoned' tea. Suddenly she shrieked! She slapped her thighs, her eyes rolled as laughter engulfed her when she saw the brown, 1.5 inch fat cockroach at the bottom of his cup. It must have dropped in during his extra shuteye.

It wasn't amusing to Clive. Revulsion occupied the whole of this face. He was greatly concerned that he may have 'picked something up' from the cockroach. We all thought it a good laugh to start the day, except Clive of course, who was a bit sulky at our mirth.

Mary was looking at her brother with some sympathy. When we left the room, she whispered to me, "Fancy leaving his cup on the floor. My dear, dear brother. He certainly needs someone to look after him". I thought of Emily and couldn't stop grinning.

The lack of real enthusiasm for the trip manifested itself in the somewhat obvious lethargic attitude adopted by Clive and Mary, which I observed with amusement. It meant that we left later than intended. I wished to reach Masindi before dark and would have to step on it if I was to succeed.

The truck had a bench seat in the front with column control, meaning we could all sit in the front of the vehicle. The road to Masindi was in quite a good condition and the fact that it was dry and dusty made things easier. The safari truck rode the corrugations very well at speed and although we had left later than intended we arrived at Masindi just as the sun was setting. We rode the rough surface through the town and booked into the hotel.

We were all happy to arrive, having travelled for about four hours, stopping to see Africa only once. Masindi was quite a busy little town, obviously flourishing with the roadside shops trading very well. Of course, they would be. It was the crossroads for trade across Lake Albert into the Congo, the northern route to Sudan and a fair amount of trade eastwards across Lake Kyoga, Soroti and onward to Nairobi, Kenya!

We were all surprised that the hotel provided such comfort. The showers just melted the dust and heat away and the drinks, good food and nice surroundings brought relaxed faces all-around. I detected a hint of enthusiasm in both Mary and Clive and thought perhaps they might possibly be looking forward to our holiday.

During conversations with the hotel staff regarding the two routes to Murchinson and various other topics, I was given the impression that the East African Railways had a big interest in the hotel or perhaps owned it. It puzzled me somewhat because the railway was nowhere near Masindi but considering the high standard experienced on the train journey from Nairobi to Kampala it could well be a probability.

In the hotel lounge during the evening, the three of us discussed which route to take to Murchinson. Mary and Clive both suggested that we take the shorter route via Kichumbanyobo. I think they wanted to get this safari over and put to bed. I told them that the hotel manager, during my discussions with him earlier in the evening, had suggested that we go via the slightly longer route (God forgive me once again my little white lies) via Butiaba. It has such fine scenic views. After that information, especially coming from the manager of the hotel they agreed to go by the latter route. I missed out the bit about it being a little more treacherous and taking a lot longer. My reasoning is whilst we are in the area, let's make the most of it and see as much as we can.

After a nourishing breakfast, we left quite early. Everyone was cheerful and weren't showing any white feathers. The northern route via Kichumbanyobo on our right was passed as we headed straight on, gradually turning west towards Butiaba and the Congo. We passed the road going to Hoima on our left and carried on through the Budongo Forest. Later, we saw four chimps retrieving something from the road ahead, but by the time we got to the spot they had vanished back into the forest.

Another rough-looking road to Hoima was seen on our left and pressing on we arrived on top of the escarpment overlooking Butiaba Port. The view was spectacular across lake Albert into the Congo, with mountains in the background. The three of us were really taken aback. The view was so beautiful and so rugged.

It was quite a dramatic descent down the escarpment and into Butiaba.

The road was damp and even with our four-wheel-drive I had to use all my driving expertise to control our descent. During our journey, Clive had not spoken very much, but Mary made up for him. She was at times like the original chatterbox. Of course, by the time Clive had worked out what he was going to say Mary probably put a shot across his bows with another bout of chatter.

During the descent, Mary ceased her chatter. I could feel the tension coming off her. She was probably holding her breath most of the time. To think I was descending into the Rift Valley once again, this time on a difficult, muddy road hundreds of miles away. I had traversed it previously on a tarmac road down the Nairobi escarpment, and also at Nakuru. How vast it was and so strange to encounter it once again on the other side of Uganda.

I think we were all relieved to get down into Butiaba. "Don't worry, we don't need to come back this way. We can come back the shorter route from Murchinson". I didn't relish the thought of driving back up the escarpment.

Butiaba was quite a busy, industrious town with a thriving cotton mill just outside the centre. Being a port on Lake Albert there was a steamboat, Thess Coryndon (named after a former Governor of Uganda from 1918 to 1922) trading with the Congo across the lake. Plus, there were numerous smaller boats and of course, many fishing boats. The place was humming with activity and it was so easy to stop awhile and take refreshment, whilst watching the town working.

Feeling thoroughly refreshed we continued up the lakeshore northwards, drinking in the most fascinating views across the lake to the Congo. The mountains in the background looked blue and were aptly named the Blue Mountains. Eventually, we arrived at Buliisa village, where we were obliged to turn east in the direction of Murchinson falls. Just a few miles north was Wanseko, a primitive fishing village right on the edge of the Nile estuary, where the Nile flowed into Lake Albert. When

I tentatively suggested that we paid it a visit I was vehemently outvoted. Perhaps Mary and Clive had thought of us being put in the cooking pot by the village inhabitants.

So, turned east we did and up to Murchinson we went. Eventually, we ran out of road and parked near an unoccupied vehicle. We now had to go on foot. The area did look wild and rough and we could hear the high cry from monkeys along with many other animal and bird noises, mostly coming from the wooded area.

"Where's the armed ranger, Cy?", said Clive. "Let us stay here until he comes." I agreed. I wanted to sit down for a little while to relax, but not in the driving seat. I received a funny odd smile from Mary when I said, "What a lovely place for a picnic!". Just then we espied four men who belonged to the other vehicle. As they approached they waved their hands in the direction from whence they had come.

"It's about a 15-minute walk to Murchinson", they said.

"Where's the armed ranger?", exclaimed Clive.

"God knows", came back the reply.

"Come on let's go for it", I said to Mary and Clive.

Mary came close and said, "I told you I wouldn't leave you for a minute". With that, she grabbed my arm and looked around the area as we walked, her head moving around like a radar antenna.

We could hear the noise coming from the falls as we approached downhill. Never have I seen anything so dramatic. The noise was deafening. Even Clive was wonderstruck. The water appeared to be boiling as the massive volume of water crashed its way through the tiny twelve foot (ish) gap. It was hard to estimate because the gorge is very wide at the top and narrows down to its base. I heard it said that it is much wider. Maybe it is now if the Nile has increased in volume!

I was very upset to hear that in 1962 Butiaba was virtually destroyed and the lake steamer was sunk by disastrous floods which played havoc in the area. If the high level of the Nile in 1962 has been maintained or partly maintained it will, of course, have reached the wider part of the gorge. I still have photographs of the falls and surrounding areas.

Whilst we were there the uniformed African game ranger came into view accompanied with a few visitors and a little African boy, who turned out to be his son. He was possibly following in his father's footsteps as a future ranger.

I wanted to take a picture from below looking up at the falls. However, beyond the falls (where the Nile flows out into a more serene and less volatile state), we could see many crocodiles languishing on the river banks about 100 feet below. Some had their mouths wide open basking in the sun. They were receiving dental flossing from white birds, which were happily picking leftover food from the crocs' teeth. The birds had no fear of entering inside their jaws. A mutual agreement was obviously with a seal of approval from the crocodiles!

I asked the ranger, "Is it possible to take a picture from below looking at the falls?".

"Not that way", he said. "It is difficult to get down there and there are many hazards including crocodiles and possibly hippos. But we can go back many meters near another fall where you can get down to base level. It does depend on how much big game is in the area and how dangerous the circumstances are."

After taking a majority 'yes' count of heads, the ranger rather reluctantly agreed to take us. He said he was concerned about the game which could be heard nearby. Mary was sticking very close to me and pulling me nearer to the ranger as we walked, which was often pulling me off balance. Clive had a numb, staring expression on his face. No word passing through his tight lips.

After about 15-minutes we came to another waterfall but the path further down to the base of the falls was blocked by many baboons. The ranger decided it was too risky to proceed.

Vic, another male member of our group and I consulted with the ranger. We decided that to compensate for our disappointment we would go across the immediate area, which we hoped would give us a better viewpoint for photographs.

"Don't you dare, Cy. Don't leave me here", exclaimed Mary.

"You'll be okay with the ranger and the rest of the party", I said. And blowing her a kiss I moved across the path to Vic. "Okay with you Ranger?"

"Oh yes, but be quick. Don't stay long." I noticed that I was not the only unpopular one, on seeing Vic receiving the silent hate gaze from his missus.

Vic and I traversed what looked like a possible trodden path, probably used by the local small wildlife. The area was covered with coarse clumps of grass interspersed with rock. As we progressed it became quieter until we could hardly hear the animal noises. We still had our friends in view. It wasn't far, yet it seemed a different atmosphere and so very, very quiet.

A little further on we saw a shallow grassy gully, yet my eyes were only on the vista I wished to photo. I went into the gully with Vic close behind me and was in the act of treading on a log as a stepping stone, when to my horror I realised almost on the point of contact, that it wasn't a log but the tail of a crocodile! The rest of its body was concealed. My foot dwelt only a second on the croc but being so abruptly roused from his siesta in the hot sun made him a bit grumpy. I leapt sideways to evade the retaliatory actions from the tail and landed on the scrubby bank, catching my cheek on a protruding rock. The croc had let loose with its tail and was moving. Vic by this time was legging it and I very soon followed. The ladies in the party screamed when they saw the croc thrashing about but stopped on seeing me emerge closely behind Vic.

I didn't lose my camera, it was wrapped around my wrist and it wasn't even damaged as it hit the rock, but I didn't get the photo either.

When we got back to the party Mary was all pent up with emotion and Clive had his head in his hands. He was not a happy soul. But Mary was soon her normal self again, pressing a handkerchief to the wound on my cheek.

The ranger said, "Pace sana' bwana" (fast move or move fast). I did not know whether he was referring to my escape or the fact that we should hurry up and move on. We all agreed to leave because it was becoming a dangerous place to be when suddenly we saw the most incredible sight. Two lionesses were being chased by a huge baboon, crossing the clearing quite close to the left of us. I could hardly believe it!

A baboon chasing a lion? Not what we have been brought up to believe. We were all fascinated by such a spectacle and traumatised with it being so close. The ranger was very alert with his rifle just in case there was a problem. He told us that this particular baboon was the powerful protector of a local group and could be very dangerous. The baboon's primary function was to protect, and as witnessed by us, he was not afraid of lions.

The ranger then told us that the area was becoming quite dangerous (as if we didn't know it) and to hurry and get back to our vehicles. Mary was holding on to me now and was very frightened and Clive still had that numb, staring expression on his face. Heeding the ranger's advice, we hightailed it back towards the vehicles. On the other side of the Nile was savannah type country with a big herd of buffalo. Needless to say, no one was tempted to explore any further.

We gave the ranger a generous tip for escorting us and also for his helpful and informative attitude. The littlun gave me a big beaming smile of lovely white teeth when I gave him something for his natural bravery for being up there with his dad. Mary very much approved of my gesture.

Clive, who was giving us all a lesson in speed walking, having taken the ranger's advice to get back to the vehicles "pace pace" (quickly) was ahead of us on his own mission. Suddenly, we heard him yelp, bend down and when he turned his face towards us it was no longer wooden. It had changed to a terrified look!

"Snake! Snake! I've been bitten by a snake!" He was holding his ankle. We surged forward to him and inspected his ankle. Sure enough, the tell-tale sign of two puncture wounds showed just above the ankle. We all gathered around, alarm and consternation registering in our group. I looked around for the snake so that I might get a description of it because it was quite vital to identify the snake so that the correct antidote could be administered at the hospital. Someone else was tying a tight bandage made up of handkerchiefs higher up Clive's leg. The ground area was covered in thick, six inch high gorse, rocks and stones. But the snake had gone and lost itself in all the cover.

The commotion attracted a South African visitor who was parked in a nice, state-of-the-art safari truck. He confidently arrived, took one look and said in his South African accent, "I got a broad-spectrum snake bite kit. I'll get eet". He went back to his truck then returned and injected Clive with the antidote. The most urgent need now was to get him to Masindi Hospital. Thanking our South African friend profusely we hightailed it out on to the Masindi Road direct via Wairingo and Igisi.

I said to Clive, "Keep calm, try to relax and don't wriggle about. The quicker your pulse and heart rate, the quicker the poison goes through your body". He was petrified and hot. Probably running a temperature! Mary was extremely worried about her brother and so was I.

"It's been a disaster, Cy, this latest thing. What a holiday! What with you almost being caught with that crocodile and now this." I was expecting her to say we shouldn't have come but she didn't oblige. She said, "Will he be okay, Cy?". What could I say? Poor old Clive was actively listening to the conversation.

I said truthfully, "It depends firstly on the South African antidote and how effective it is, what type of snake it was, and what time we get to this hospital. It's a pity we didn't catch a glimpse of the snake".

We delivered Clive to Masindi Hospital in record time. He was quickly seen when we told them it was a snake bite. They were a bit upset when told we could not describe the snake, then became happier when I told them about the South African broad-spectrum antidote. They whisked him away and left Mary and I to sit and worry about him. We sat down and Mary gave a big sigh.

"I'll be glad to get home, Cy. I'm not cut out for all this dangerous life!"

"I promise, Mary I will sit in my slippers from now on."

Mary gave me a disbelieving smile and said, "I'm sure I will".

Eventually, a nursing sister came out and said, "It seems the South African antidote has been effective and although the bite was serious it was not a life-threatening case!".

Clive was given medication to calm him down and stayed on the bed for a couple of hours before being delivered back into our care. Because it was late and therefore dark, it was a slower run back to Kampala. On the return journey, I pulled up in the dark. Neither Mary nor Clive wished to see Africa, so I decided to get out myself.

"Don't get out in the dark!", said Mary. "It might not be safe."

"No problem, pet. I'm not going to stray. I'll promise to stay by the nearest tyre." I was curious that neither of them wished to go. I soon returned and we continued on our way.

A while later Clive suddenly blurted out, "I'm desperate to see Africa and I don't mind telling you that I am scared of getting out in the dark".

"Me too!", quickly chirped Mary.

"That's okay," I said. "No cause for alarm, there's a large tin can in the back for this type of situation." (Plastic was not in the vocabulary then.)

Clive said, "It is so disgusting, primitive and embarrassing. I should never have agreed to come in the first place".

"You can always pee out of the rear door Clive."

"God, this is dreadful", he said as he scrambled over the seat.

Jokingly I said, "Don't make too much noise Clive!!". I received a somewhat abrasive reply.

He had the rear door open as he relieved himself. Mary whispered "I am sorry Clive is so naïve and so straight-laced, but I am embarrassed as well as Clive in this situation! Not with you! It's just with my brother being present".

"Forget about him. He's just a prude."

"I'm definitely not getting out of the truck, Cy." She said this with a certain amount of authority, most probably to overcome her shyness.

"I'll come with you, pet."

"Not even with you, Cy. I just don't know where we are in this God-forsaken wilderness and I don't know what is lurking out there. I'll pee in this tin bucket and be damned because I can't wait much longer."

Clive returned. "Everything okay now, Clive?" I did not get a reply but got a dig in the ribs from Mary as she turned to scrabble over the seat. After a short interval, I heard the continuous tinkle reverberating in the tin bucket and thought of Anne. She would have thought it a huge joke. It would not have concerned her one bit. Clive gave a slight snort and covered his ears with his hands, obviously embarrassed. I felt a little sorry for him, as dear old Mary was happily tinkling away feeling considerably better as the seconds ticked by. Once Mary had returned to her seat we set off on the road to Kampala once again.

Then I started with a fit of the giggles. I think it was Clive's attitude which brought it on, plus Mary's tinkling sound and my imagination running away with itself. I was visualising Mary trying to balance on a can half the size of a bucket.

Hearing me trying to stifle my giggling set Mary off giggling. She kept digging me in the side hoping to stop me but it didn't. Mary went into really serious giggling.

"It's nothing to laugh about", said Clive. That made it worse and more audible. Tears were running down my cheeks, likewise, Mary's because she was dabbing at her eyes. It took some little time to become normal once again.

The lights of Kampala came into view and shortly afterwards we were outside Mary's flat on Nakasero Hill. As soon as the door opened there was an orderly dash to the loo.

When Clive said goodnight, I didn't ask him if he had enjoyed his holiday. But I did wonder what could possibly cure his strange attitude to life. Perhaps a good woman? Yes, that could be it. A good woman or on second thoughts, a thoroughly bad one would be better!

EPILOGUE

After Clive had departed homeward and Mary and I had settled into a more sober routine, I received a most exciting letter. It offered me the post of 'District Engineering Officer' (DEO) for Entebbe District. I was over the moon! Being in charge of my own district! It was to me, the ultimate goal of my career and above all, it was Entebbe District, the most prestigious post one could wish for. However, it did have a heavy responsibility to match, both technically and administratively.

Being in charge of my own district I would, of course, be on undefined hours, but that could be a double-edged sword so to speak. I could have little to do and have a siesta whenever I wished, or I might have to work all the hours that God has given us, the latter being assuredly so. Many vital aspects would have to be assessed. The array of highly technical installations contained in the district in addition to the corresponding degree of maintenance would not allow much free time.

Many of the aforementioned technical installations were associated with the airport and would be urgent and very high priority. Entebbe airport being an international airport had major airline companies claiming priority. Entebbe also had an automatic exchange and like Granddad was getting on a bit and would need help, tender loving care and time. Propping up and keeping going elderly equipment was fast becoming a primary function. The airport also had a private automatic exchange which would also be my responsibility.

The seat of the Ugandan government was based at Entebbe, so the secretariat with all its departments would expect a high standard of service. His Excellency, the Governor of Uganda, at Government House (representing Her Majesty the Queen), had his own specialised equipment and most assuredly would be on my back.

I would have to sit on committees, listening to the usual time-wasting waffle. All the normal external telephone communication of the district would be my ultimate responsibility. But hopefully I would have trained Asian and African staff to deal with that aspect.

The district administration would include payment of my staff and their welfare, vehicles and their maintenance and evaluation of stores (both technical and non-technical). The thought of the colossal amount of correspondence and files involved in running the district filled me with dread!

I would have a budget to adhere to, amounting to a considerable amount of money, divided into many sections, detailing the limit I could spend in each section. Each year I would be required, after stocktaking, to submit estimates for each section and a total budget for the next financial year, for approval by the Crown Agents in London.

That was a simple summary of the main aspects of the running of my district.

I really appreciated the final part viz. 'I will, if I accept the appointment, be expected to cover the requirement of the district 24 hours a day, 7 days a week'. I.e. I would be on permanent emergency call, yet above all, I would have the freedom to run my own district, hopefully with a good staff. In reality, I would be married to the district.

I knew that I would accept it. I couldn't resist the challenge. Think of the prestige I would lose if I didn't! Mary was over the moon when I told her. She was highly delighted for me. She said, "I'm so very proud of you, Cy". Then jumping up, laughing and acting the fool, she sang 'My man's the DEO'. She did some walking up and down the lounge, wearing a snobbish look on her face. She was so happy now. It was so good to see her this way.

Sitting down after her bit of fun, she wrinkled her brow and said, "I'm so very thrilled and excited by it all, but what about my job in Kampala?".

"Luckily you work for a government department. It will be easy to arrange for you to be transferred to Entebbe."

She was still excited and wide-eyed. "Think of all the garden parties at Government House. And my hats and dresses, I can't wait to tell everyone. We will only be 21 miles from Kampala so we can still keep our friends." She paused, thinking for a moment then said, "There is one thing, Cy".

"Oh, what is that?" I thought she is so excited she can't keep still and her thoughts and questions must be queuing up.

"Well…" she said, "You will lose your identity, won't you?". Then she carried on before I could reply. "You will be like the Aide-De-Camp to the Governor. Everyone calls him the ADC and not a lot of us remember his name. People will say 'That's the DEO' or 'Here comes the DEO'. Not 'That's Cy' or 'Here comes Cy'."

"I'll let you call me Cy if you are very good and if you promise to behave yourself." That started a rough and tumble with a cushion fight which finished on the floor with Mary victorious, of course. Both of us ended up hot and breathless. We were feeling the humidity before the 'aggression'.

A few days later we went to see our new home. It was out of the Entebbe township on a murram road by the shore of Lake Victoria. It was quite a long, old timber bungalow. But its position or setting was the opposite of a conventional dwelling. There was no front door on the roadside. It was situated on the opposite side which was the lakeside where it opened onto a long veranda which ran the whole length of the building. All the rooms leading from it. The rear of the building faced the road where the dhobi (washing) room and houseboy quarters were. These areas were joined to the main structure by a covered, open-air walkway with expanded metal strands in place of windows.

There were no gates nor fences. There was just a rough murram drive from the road at one end of the bungalow, culminating in a circle at the front of the building facing the lake. Thus enabling you to drive in and out of the property without having to reverse.

Between the house and the lake was a distance of 200 yards comprising of elephant grass infested with snakes and mini wildlife. Hippopotamuses were known to come up to the bungalow and wander around the area at night. It was too far for crocodiles — what a shame!

An African village was almost next door where watoto waved to us as we passed by. I should imagine that it could be quite a noisy establishment on occasions, with drums and vocal celebrations, with hopefully happy, friendly neighbours.

The most rewarding factor was the uninterrupted view over the lake, with a few small islands on the extreme left, in the Port Bell direction. The lake, being so huge, was tidal and mimicked the sea by disappearing over the horizon.

I pondered about the future. What was I taking on? Would I be able to cope? And Mary, would she be able to stand up to the demanding pace, the expected emergency call outs and the very nature of my position also having unknown intrusion into our present way of life.

Mary thought it was a dream come true, "Our own lovely place, Cy. But we'll have to watch out for snakes! I was thinking about emergency call outs in the middle of the night, with possibly grumpy hippos for company, but kept those happy thoughts to myself. I didn't want to spoil the moment, yet I could already feel the possibility of more mayhem!

We stood outside the bungalow side by side, our arms around each other's waists, looking across the shimmering water into the boiling hot sun. We were two miles north of the equator in the middle of Africa. I was looking forward to this new challenge, yet with a touch of apprehension.

Excited? Yes! And both of us utterly happy and content. DEO Entebbe. Another funny, exciting and interesting phase of my life.

But that's another story!

ABOUT THE AUTHOR

Cy was born on Good Friday 13th, 1923. He lived through the Blitz and at 17 years old served with the Home Guard. Later, he joined the Fleet Air Arm throughout the wartime period described in his first book, *Mayhem in France*. On return to civilian life he became a Senior Technical Officer in telecommunications.

In 1950, Cy was accepted into Her Majesty's Colonial Service before being seconded to the East African High Commission. Cy served in Kenya and Uganda until 1962. The adventures in this book took place between 1950 and 1955, at which point he was appointed as the District Engineering Officer — a position of high esteem. The latter African period is being woven into his future and third title, *Mayhem in Entebbe*.

Returning to the UK in 1962, he designed and built a mushroom farm in North West Devon. Ably assisted by his very close friend and confidant, Margaret R Collings, Cy sold mushrooms to the wholesale market for 20 years. Over 12 years during the same period he spent his spare time forming and maintaining the well-known Woolsery Youth Club.

In 1989 Cy embarked on the world cruise liner *Canberra*, where he met his lovely wife, Ursula. On returning to the UK, they settled down in the sleepy village of Kingskerswell in South Devon.

Cy writes during the dark winter evenings in a comfy chair with a pen and a pad. It is the only way he writes, just as it happened, such a long time ago.